"Haske describes Michigan's Upper Peninsula so vividly that you can hear the birches bend in the relentless winter wind, catch a whiff of a muskrat edging along a lake, and feel the icy sludge pack beneath weathered boots. More striking than his talent for displaying the harsh northern landscape, though, is an astonishing gift for exposing the bleak terrain of the desperate heart throbbing against relentless challenges of hard times and hard places, of hard luck and hard work. Read this novel for lessons in how to survive, lessons in how to thrive, and lessons in how to write!"

—Ron Cooper, Author of *Purple Jesus* and *Hume's Fork*

"Joseph Daniel Haske's world is hardscrabble as hell, and if you're like me, you won't want to leave. A favorite diner smells of Clorox and lard, and the truck bed stinks of trash bags full of freshly dipped smelt. But damn if things don't taste good. Damn if there isn't always another couple cans of beer or a pint of Kessler's to chase down a Fat Frankie or settle some bad nerves after you've been tossed from a place because you don't know how to act in public. Damn if Haske's able hands don't make the U.P. a world I recognize instantly and I've never been there. Place is the necessary angel in *North Dixie Highway* and that Yooper dude's wings, flapping through these pages, just off the water, make a rough music, a song that stinks true because Haske made it so."

—Steve Davenport, Author of *Uncontainable Noise* and *Overpass*

"*North Dixie Highway* is a taut, understated narrative featuring a working-class American back from the wars in the former Yugoslavia. Suffering through emotional distress, the young veteran conflates the cruel violence of war with a long-time family feud. Many of the strongest scenes are descriptive: the rural areas around Michigan's Upper Peninsula and the war-rendered wasteland of Bosnia. Joseph Haske has written a tensely restrained novel that vibrates in the mind well after reading."

—Harold Jaffe, Author of *Revolutionary Brain*, *OD*, and *Anti-Twitter*

"A redneck Jim Harrison, J.D. Haske writes with a blue-collar poet's sensibilities, replacing pretentiousness with tension, and creating a world where north meets south, vet meets civilian, and all is slowly changed forever."

—Ron Riekki, Author of *U.P.: a novel* and *The Way North: Collected Upper Peninsula New Works*

North Dixie Highway

Joseph D. Haske

Texas Review Press • Huntsville, Texas

North Dixie Highway
Joseph D. Haske
Texas Review Press · Huntsville, Texas

Printed in the United States of America

Acknowledgments: I would like to give special thanks to all of my readers, especially Richard, Paul, Daniel, Robin, Liana, Rob, and Judy.
Excerpts of this book have appeared in *Boulevard*, *Pleiades*, the *Texas Review*, *Romania Literara*, *Convorbire Literare*, *Alecart*, *Rampike*, *Fiction International,* the *Four-Way Review*, and *Border Crossing*.

To the editors of these journals, I am forever grateful.

Author photo: Richard Coronado
Cover photo: Barbie Lee
Book cover design: Daniel M. Mendoza

Library of Congress Cataloging-in-Publication Data

Haske, Joseph D.
North Dixie Highway / Joseph D. Haske.
pages cm
ISBN 978-1-937875-26-8 (pbk. : alk. paper)
I. Title.
PS3608.A78986N67 2013
813'.6--dc23

2013017340

For family, especially my grandparents: Myles, Mary, Edlore, Ramona, and Bill.

North Dixie Highway

If the red slayer think he slays,
Or if the slain think he is slain,
They know not well the subtle ways
I keep, and pass, and turn again

-Ralph Waldo Emerson

PROLOGUE

A vision borne in 1914, the Dixie Highway was never a specific freeway or thoroughfare, but more of a series of roads, some paved, many not, built to connect remote areas and cities throughout a large section of the eastern United States; it brought together rural areas from south to north and enabled the growth of commerce, easing transportation and access. From Miami, through wetlands, swamp and citrus groves, through Ocala's thoroughbred fields and north to red clay and Georgia pines, through South Carolina forests and the Blue Ridge mountains of North Carolina, Dixie Highway routes stretched into Tennessee mountains and Kentucky hills and over Midwest flatlands, the corn and wheat fields of Ohio, Indiana, Illinois and southern Michigan. The roadways reached up into Chicago and looped around Michigan's lower peninsula, peaking, for a time, in Mackinaw City, and having gone that far, the vision would later extend to the Canadian border, through the eastern Upper Peninsula, the most remote section of land touched by the Dixie Highway system.

They ferried man and machine over four miles across the narrowest stretch of the Straits of Mackinac, over the frigid waters where Lake Huron meets Lake Michigan, with no expansion bridge in 1919 to connect the peninsulas. The north most section of the eastern division of the Dixie Highway was almost an afterthought, a stretch of road from the south shore of the lakes that stopped dead at St. Mary's rapids in the dark frosted shadows of the north, a land connected to Ontario by a single railway bridge. In the land of the Algonquin, where travelers met for centuries and the locals fished the lakes and rivers, Clay Steven Taylor, a Tennessee foreman working on the Dixie Highway project near Sault Ste. Marie was murdered by an Irish immigrant named Teddy Cronin, the only serious casualty associated with highway construction during the U.P. expansion. Witnesses say Cronin struck a blow to the back of Taylor's head with a shovel and absconded with thirty dollars, Taylor's gold watch and wedding ring. The company was ordered to pay Taylor's widow eighty-five dollars cash as compensation and the rest of the road crew was offered an undisclosed bonus to remain silent regarding the work-related accident. Cronin's wife Brigit, by some workers' personal accounts, was pregnant with Taylor's son.

1994

With every mile Johnny drives, Lester Cronin is closer to dead. Nobody knows this yet but me. Nobody ever talks about what happened to Grandpa Eddie anymore, like the whole family just forgot all about it, but I never will. The last four years, my whole time in the Army, I've been planning and working toward revenge, waiting for the chance to set things right. Once I finish off Lester, I'll go to college on the G.I. Bill—move on and live a respectable life. But I'm coming home to take care of business first.

Officially I'm on active duty until September, but I had enough leave time left to out-process two months early. Dad and Johnny picked me up at Detroit Metro in Johnny's Delta 88 five hours ago. We get the first view of the bridge coming up from I-75 and the sky stretches out around the ivory suspension arches. The blue from the lakes blends and melts together with the sky, reaching up toward the clouds and the gulls. Our windows are down and the damp, dense air tastes cool and fresh, not like the south Georgia summer heat I just left.

Dad sits in the middle of the backseat, crowded in by Johnny's blue sweatpants, duffel bags and two pairs of basketball shoes. Johnny got a scholarship to play at Hillsdale but he spends the summer at home, up north with the rest of the family. There's only three beers left in the case of Busch that Dad bought at the Shell station in Pontiac. He cracks one for himself and passes another up to me.

"Bet you'd like one of these, eh Johnny?"

Johnny jerks the wheel just hard enough to wet Dad's t-shirt with Busch.

"Colonel Henry ain't doing so good," Dad says. "The hard life's finally catching up with him. Walks with a cane now."

"What's he, ninety-two?" Johnny asks.

"Ninety-four in November," Dad says.

"Might still have a good run left in him," I say.

"Looks rough since the last time you seen him, Buck," Dad says. "Something in his eyes, like the fight just ain't there."

"I'll never count Henry down till he's out for good," I say.

"Your Grandma Clio's doing great, though," he says. "Women get the better end."

Grandma Clio's a good thirty years younger than Henry and she had a rough time keeping up with him until a few years ago.

Didn't see Grandma Clio or Henry last year when I came up for Christmas. Spent Christmas Eve with Grandma Gloria. The old two-story farm house looked more faded and beat-up than I remembered. The white outside walls are stained with time and weather and the barn is in even worse shape—a cold wind blowing down from Ontario would take it down. It was good to see family but it's not the same as it used to be. Dad's side of the family used to be close, now everybody's doing their own thing. Cousin Gwen spent Christmas Eve with her boyfriend's family, something nobody would've done when Grandpa was alive. After Grandma downed her fifth shot of Kessler's she told Aunt Alexa that Gwen could forget about spending next Christmas Eve with the family. Even if she begged, she wouldn't let Gwen in the house.

There's not much room in the old house anyway, with all the new grandkids running around. It's a big enough house for a regular family, but not for us Metzgers. It gets really loud with all the little shits running around the house with jingle bells and crying to open their presents. I had to step outside every ten minutes or so just to clear my head. Right before dinner, Dad, Uncle Karl, and me all sat out on the porch a good half hour in sixteen degrees and wind. Passed around the Seagram's and chopped beef till they called us in for dinner at ten. Uncle Karl couldn't hardly walk by then and the raw beef and cracker crumbs were frozen to his moustache. Aunt Julie was so embarrassed she grabbed him by the ear and drug him into the back room. Later on, Karl kept telling me, "See what happens when you get married? Don't do it, Buck." He must've said it about twelve times and Julie kept giving him that look like he murdered her sister or something. Bet Karl got it good back home. Sure as hell didn't get laid.

We're still a half hour from the house but I can taste the cedars and the evergreens, the fresh Lake Huron water. Down below Johnny's side of the bridge is Fort Michilimackinac and on my side the public access beach, at least a hundred people running around with coolers, barbecue, beach balls and beer. There's sailboats and freight ships under the bridge where Lake Huron meets Lake Michigan and the ferries spray white foam from their engines on the route to Mackinac Island.

"Ever wonder why the Mackinaw is spelled with a "W" in Mackinaw City and every time you see Mackinac on the other side of the bridge, it's spelled with a 'C'?"

"It's so the Buckeyes, Fudgies, and Trolls learn how to say it right fore they cross the bridge," says Dad.

I've been a lot of places in the last four years and there's nothing so clean, nothing so green, blue and fresh as the U.P. shoreline. There's a few less people up here now than when I was a kid, but the population's pretty much been the same for a hundred years. In some towns around here, like ours, they got no-franchise laws. It keeps everything like it was in the old days, but there's not many new jobs and no new business. When I was a kid, places like St. Ignace seemed big, but across the bridge all we'll see is a town smothered in spruce and birch, no city sprawl, just small blue and white houses scattered in dark green hills.

"See that cement support there," says Dad. "There's a body in there. Under the tower. Mason fell in when they were pouring cement. Nothing they could do but keep on pouring. My old man worked with a guy, Steve Pitt. He seen it happen."

Dad's been moonlighting—working construction and down at the loading docks again. There's been steady work there for a few years now. When me and Johnny were kids, he used to do a lot of odd jobs on the side. For a couple years, he worked the woods steady. He'd pay Johnny and me five dollars each to go with him and trim the limbs off the big trees with a bow saw and then stack the firewood. One summer he was working out by Bear Creek. Johnny and me would bring our poles and flies and go after trout when we finished the firewood. A couple times, Dad even joined us when the chainsaw dulled. That's the first time he really started talking to us. Mom always said you could never shut him up before he got drafted. He mostly talked to Uncle Tony after the war, but with Tony gone, guess he went back to his old self.

"It's your first day of freedom. We should keep this buzz going. Hit the Skunk House or the Channel Marker. It's still happy hour."

"Maybe we should get back and see everybody," I tell him.

"Your Mom's working till later and your little brother Tommy's fishing with your uncle Karl. You'll see everybody else soon enough. Plenty of time."

"We should go to the casino," says Johnny.

"How you gonna get in?" Dad asks him. "You ain't twenty-one yet."

"What casino?" I ask.

"I got it covered," Johnny tells Dad.

"There's casinos up here now. At the reservations," says Dad. He grabs Johnny by the sweatshirt sleeve. "Where did you get a fake ID you little son-of-a-bitch?" Dad lifts his hand to cuff him but he slaps his own knee and starts to laugh. "Just like your old man," he tells Johnny.

We take the scenic route through St. Ignace, downtown, past the bus stop where I left for the Army almost four years ago. We stop at the IGA for a twelve pack and sandwiches.

"Just enough to get us there," says Dad. "They got free drinks in the casino. Made it past the bridge—guess you can have a couple now," he tells Johnny.

Johnny cracks his second Busch by the time we pass the exit for home. He keeps the Oldsmobile on a straight course north to the Sault.

When I was nineteen, we did a training mission out in Death Valley, California, at the NTC. It was my second trip out there. First time we flew, the second time we came back on buses. We stopped in Vegas for a few hours and most of the guys hit the casinos or the whorehouses. Since I was a minor, I couldn't get into the casinos, but there were slot machines everywhere. I played slot machines at a McDonalds and a couple in a gas station. Sergeant Sullivan said it wasn't a problem unless I won a big jackpot, then I'd need somebody to claim it for me. If that happened, he said we'd split it. I never hit the three lines. Lost my last twenty-five bucks, except for a quarter. I bet that last quarter and won back five bucks. Didn't push my luck from there, cause it was enough to get food. When the buses lined up to leave for Georgia, Sergeant Morgan didn't make it back to the convoy in time. They said he was with some red-haired midget prostitute. Next time we saw him he was Private Morgan.

The Sault casino is darker than the ones in Vegas, but there's enough glass and bright lights to make it glow purple in the night sky. The hotel that's connected is bigger than any I've seen in this city, even though it's half the size of the smaller Vegas casino hotels. The electric beams around the lower section light the outer doors like gold.

"Who's feeling the luck tonight?" Dad asks.

"I'm gonna tell you guys something, but don't get pissed," says Johnny.

He shows us the fake ID and it's my real drivers license that I thought I lost two summers ago when we were swimming out at Detour State Park.

"You little cocksucker." I grab his collar and Dad grabs my arm.

"What's done's done," says Dad. "Johnny, you're gonna sit your ass in the car a good hour, then you try to get in. Can't have two people with the same name and birthday come in at the same time. You get arrested, we ain't bailing you out till we got our fill of free drinks, got it—dumbass."

The casino is bigger inside than I thought it would be. Except for the cigarette smoke, it smells clean and new, like cedar and carpet shampoo. The floor is red, gold, flat and hard. The entry looks like the fancy hotels where we had our battalion Christmas parties. Instead of dress blues there's workers all around in their white shirts and dark red bowties. Most of the gamblers wear t-shirts, ball caps, jeans and flannels. The security guard stares at my ID and looks back at my face a few times before he lets us in. Johnny might have a problem when he tries to get in. There's animal mounts all around the front area and a statue of a Chippewa warrior next to some steel-framed display cases with old black and white pictures of Ojibwa

Indians fishing the St. Mary's. Besides that, it's not much different than the Vegas casinos, what I saw from the lobbies.

"Let's hit the Blackjack table," Dad says. "Slot machines are for suckers. Don't tell the old lady, but I lost my overtime check on those quarter slots last week. Least with Blackjack you got a fighting chance."

Soon as we sit down, there's Johnny at the side of the Blackjack table.

"Told you to wait a while," says Dad.

"It's cool. Heather works here. Saw her coming in for her shift and we walked in together from a side door. Lend me a couple twenties. I'll double it in an hour."

"I'll give you twenty. Only got forty here. Need to hit the ATM."

Dad and I both change twenty and bet the two dollar minimum. Johnny goes straight to a dollar machine. It's not long before Dad's down to his last four bucks. He gets a pair of sevens and the dealer's showing a four.

"Split 'em," he tells the dealer. He draws fours on both. "I need to double down on these," he tells me. "Johnny, give me back my twenty, you motherfucker," he yells out toward the dollar slots. Johnny doesn't hear with Bob Seger cranking from the lounge speakers and the rings, rhythms and clicks of the dollar machines."

"Sir, we're gonna need you to calm down," says the dealer. He waves in the security guard.

"What you need, four bucks? Here." I slide the tokens toward him.

"Sir, there's no exchange of tokens at the table. This is your warning."

Dad cracks his knuckles. "I see how it is. You don't want me to double down. Just hit 'em you little prick."

The fat security guard with greasy hair taps Dad on the shoulder. "You're cut off sir. Any more language like that and we're gonna have to ask you to leave."

Dad draws a jack and an eight. The dealer busts. "You motherfucker," Dad says. "I should've won double."

The security guard grabs Dad's shirt collar and jerks him out of his chair. Three more security guards come running over. Dad's chair falls to the gold and red squares on the carpet and his beer pours out onto the green blackjack table felt.

"Look what you done," says the female security guard. "Get his ass out of here before I call the cops."

"He didn't do shit. It was your boy here," I tell her.

"You need to leave too," she tells me.

"What did I do?" She doesn't answer. I look at the dealer and he just looks away. "You can't do this—it's not right," I say.

"Are you gonna leave the premise or do we need to escort you out?"

"Check the cameras," I say. The dealer and guards ignore me.

I grab what's left of my tokens and join Dad in the parking lot. Johnny's nowhere around. The fat-ass guard and the other one who kicked out Dad are still walking back to the door.

"I'll be seeing you around, you fat bitch," I tell him. He reaches for his club but the other guard stops him.

"I'll be looking for you," he tells me. His body starts to shake but he's not afraid. Wants to prove something here and now.

"Go sober up," says the other one. "It's not worth it," he tells the fat guard. "They're not worth it."

One night, down in Columbus, Georgia, a couple fat-fuck bouncers like this guy kicked my friend Doug out of Ernie's Roadhouse. Opened the door with Doug's head. Me, Roberts, Morgan, Diaz and Rizzoli waited till they closed up and we followed one of the bouncers to his apartment. We put his bald head through the window of his own Camaro. His scalp was hamburger by the time the glass cracked and shattered. He curled up on the sidewalk like a baby and just started crying.

When all the apartment lights started coming on, I thought we'd be busted for sure but we squealed out in Rizzoli's truck just when somebody opened the door and started yelling at us. My chest got real tight and I had a hard time breathing. My hand was cut and bleeding from the glass from the bouncer's Camaro. We passed a state trooper on the way back to Fort Benning, and I thought for sure we'd get pulled over. Somebody must've seen the truck and the plates. By the time we got back, my buzz was gone and I couldn't sleep. I haven't slept right since. The bouncer had it coming. I never felt bad about what we did. It's just scary to think how easy it is for somebody to come after you when you don't expect it.

That's how it is too, like that kid in Bosnia, Samson. He was alert to everything in the field, but he didn't see it coming when that fuel truck ran him over. A few feet here or there, could've been any one of our sleeping bags. There's just too much shit like that to think about. Most the time, I have to drink myself to sleep if I can sleep at all. Then I wake up sudden like the time the blue Kevlar fell from the ammo shelf in that Bradley, right on my forehead and damned near knocked me unconscious. I'm shaking good now, and breathing heavy, but it's not fear—more like the opposite.

Dad and I wait by the car for a good half hour but Johnny never comes out.

"Let's get a drink," Dad says.

There's still a mismatched seven pack of Busch and Old Milwaukee in the backseat of Johnny's car but we don't have the keys. We walk out to the gas station across the road from the parking lot. Dad wants Kessler's but they don't sell liquor.

"Let's go into town and get a pint," he says. "We ain't got nothing better to do."

It's at least a couple miles to downtown, but we head out into the dark down Shunk Road.

"Your Ma gets home in an hour," Dad tells me. "Gonna be pissed we're not there yet."

"Maybe the casino wasn't such a good idea," I tell him. "Johnny might be in there all night. What's that on your arm?" It's the first time I notice the blood on his sleeve. It looks purple on his faded red t-shirt.

"Must've happened when that fat fuck pushed me out the door. He's lucky I'm so drunk or I would've kicked his ass."

"We could give him some payback."

"I'm listening."

"When we get back to the casino parking lot, we'll stake out the place, figure out what car is his. Then we -"

"I ain't sitting around all night trying to find his car. Loser like that ain't worth that kind of payback. Should've knocked his ass out in the parking lot. That's what he deserves."

It's not too long before we come up on a party store. There's no houses around, just the flashing neon sign and a flood light in front of a garage door. Looks like someone just turned an old house into a store. The purple-green light from a bug zapper shines over the rotted screen door entrance.

"Evening, gentlemen," says a white-haired lady with brown oval frames. She's only about five foot two but must weigh close to two hundred pounds.

"Hey there," says the old man. "Don't suppose you got a pint of Kessler's for me?"

"It's Saturday night. Sold out the pints but I got a fifth if that'll do you."

Dad grabs a brown paper bag of venison jerky and a box of Swishers. The lady puts it all in a bigger brown bag with the fifth. Dad snags his red t-shirt on the screen door latch. It rips a good size hole before the door springs back against the frame. It echoes like a rifle shot over the field and the neon sign shakes above us.

We finish off more than half the Kessler's by the time we make it to the St. Mary's river, ducking into alleys and side streets along the way for shots. Somehow we end up on Portage between the Edison plant and the country club.

"We should probably head back and find Johnny," I say.

"Let's take a break here. Just for five minutes," Dad says. He starts walking toward a bench when a blue Chevy Silverado pulls up.

"William, is that really you?"

Most people who know me call me Buck. A handful of friends call me Billy or Billy Buck. Only people who ever called me William were Great Grandma Aideen, Mrs. Gurov and Stacey Larson.

"What are you doing out here, William?"

"Came with Johnny. He's still at the casino. The old man and I got tired of Blackjack so we took a walk. What are you doing?"

"Dinner at the club. They asked me to play in a quintet. Hey, you guys want a ride somewhere?"

"Which way you headed?"

"Just on my way home. Kind of hungry though. Want to grab some food?"

"Alright." Dad's slouched over the park bench. I help him to the truck.

"Is he okay? You guys had a few," Stacey says when she gets a good whiff.

"It's those free drinks at the casino," Dad says.

Mom must be back from work by now. She'll be pissed off for sure that we're not home, but we can't do much about it since Johnny's our ride. More than anybody, Mom was there for me while I was on active duty, sending me letters and helping with all my business back home. Last time I talked to her, it was from a phone booth in Columbus. The whole time I was riled up, trying to handle the idea of going back to civilian life. She was trying to calm me down with all her logic, but I just got more frustrated. She put up with me until I mentioned getting payback for Grandpa Eddie, then she told me I was acting just like him and Lester Cronin so I hung up. When we get home, I'll try to explain everything—that it wasn't her, just the stress. Then I'll never mention what I'm thinking again. People don't seem to like the truth much, especially mothers.

Stacey wanted to eat at the Palace but it was too full, so we decided to go across the street to Frank's Diner. Dad's passed out in the truck. "Just let me rest a couple minutes," he told us three times. "Then I'll come in for a burger." He's done for the night.

We cross the street by Maloney's and turn left toward Frank's. There's a group of young stoners in flannels and black sock caps. Must be college guys, but they're trying to act gangster. They eye up Stacey when we walk past. The one with the nose piercing gives me a bad look. I feel their stares from behind us until we get to the glass door of the diner. It's hot inside. Steam rolls out from the kitchen. A table of old men laugh over the clanking pots and pans and the clinks of real glass cups. There's a yellow wet floor sign just past the door mat and our shoes stick to the stained white tile when we walk up to the hostess. There's lard and Clorox in the air and I taste it mixing with the damp summer heat from the fan while the brunette in a short black dress walks us to a booth.

"Ever eat here before?" Stacey asks me. She sniffs in the greasy air of the place and cringes.

"All the time before I left. Food's great here."

"Just be the two of you," the hostess says. She's cute but has a pudgy face and braces that make her look younger when she smiles.

Her brown hair is tucked into a dark hair net and her acne is bright red on her greasy face.

"Your dad okay out there? I feel bad," Stacey says.

"That's what you get when you pass out early in my family."

"He looked really tired. Didn't get much sleep?"

The waitress sets down two glasses of ice water and two plastic-covered menus.

"They got up early to pick me up at Detroit," I tell her. Truth is, it's the Kessler's that knocked him out. I'm tired as hell too, but I can't sleep lately. Last three days, I slept one hour.

"What'll you have?" the blonde waitress asks. She's about Mom's age and looks familiar. With our family you never know.

"I'll have the Fat Frankie," I say. Stacey squints at me.

"Great choice," says the waitress.

"Sounds real healthy," Stacey says, "but I'll have the roasted turkey, I guess."

"Nothing wrong with a Fat Frankie," I tell her when the waitress walks toward the kitchen.

"So you just got back today," Stacey says. "How does it feel to be a free man again?"

Stacey's eyes are hungry and locked into mine but they're glossier than I noticed till now. She must've had a few drinks at the club or maybe toked it up with the other musicians. I'm a couple years older than her, but we used to hang out. Met her at a baseball game about ten years ago. Her brother Ben was the catcher on my team, little league through high school, ever since they moved here from Marquette. I kissed Stacey at a party in high school and she even wrote me a few letters when I was gone, but not much ever came of it. Something will come out of this situation, though, the way she's looking at me.

"I saw Blake Braune the other day," she tells me. "Asked me if I knew how you were doing. I didn't realize you'd be getting out so soon."

"Me either," I tell her. "I took all the leave time I had left so I could get back in time for the fall semester. How's Blake? Only seen him once in the last four years."

Most people think Blake and I are close since we played on the same teams together, hung out with the same crowd. Truth is,

I haven't been thinking much about him or the old crowd for the last couple of years. The platoon brothers were my family while I was gone.

"I don't see Blake much, she says. Seems fine. Last week I had to pick up a hammer for my dad at Cronin's hardware and I ran into him and Jason."

"That place is still open? I was kind of hoping they burned it down by now." She gives me a funny look and I realize she doesn't know the rumors about Lester Cronin killing Grandpa Eddie. She doesn't know how much I hate old man Cronin so she must think I'm crazy. The name Cronin makes all the hair on my body stand up and I feel a tingling over my scalp. We don't say a word until the waitress comes back with our plates. Stacey might still be looking at me the same way, but I can't focus on her eyes. Faraway places and people and times I'll never see again flash through my mind. Sitting down at the booth made my buzz more intense and the room starts to spin around us.

"Here's your dinner," says the waitress. "You want light mayo for that turkey?"

"How about mustard?" Stacey asks.

The waitress nods. "Be right back with that. Enjoy."

Stacey stares down my Fat Frankie and fake gags before she smiles at me.

"Hey, this is good shit," I tell her. "Want to try it?"

"I don't eat red meat," she says.

"Your loss. Don't tell me you don't like a good burger once in a while."

"When I was a kid. Now it just makes me sick to think about it. Red meat comes from smart animals. Chickens and turkeys don't feel as much pain, right?"

It's the kind of bullshit we tell ourselves to justify our stupid theories about life. It's the kind of lie we tell to sleep better at night. Most people don't bother calling other people's bullshit for a lot of reasons. I'd be stupid to call bullshit when a beautiful girl like Stacey looks at me the way she's looking at me now, so what I tell her is, "You might be right."

Her lips curl. I feel her leg brush mine under the table. She reaches out to touch my arm and it calms me as much as I can calm.

There's a loud noise from the kitchen, like the chop of an axe or the sound of a mortar fragment on metal. I jump up from the booth enough to bang my right knee on the wood. First she looks at me, scared, then we both laugh like it's some kind of joke. I feel the cold in my chest and sweat over my whole body while I nod and watch those beautiful red lips move.

1983

It's open war in Grandpa's driveway, man against bird. So far, Grandpa Eddie don't need help. Man, that old guy can swing an axe. Never seen nothing like it, the way blood shoots out little white chicken necks and paints the limestone. There's still two, three running round, no heads, every time he pins another one down on the elm stump. If chickens had souls, they might look like the steam spilling out their necks to the frost. The killing part ain't all that bad but I got a empty stomach and I puked up in my mouth twice. Death is the worst smell. Even chicken death makes the rotten garbage in a summertime dumpster smell sweet. My eyes water with the cold air and the gas from all them carcasses. Every time I catch a fresh whiff, I gag. Really something to see the way Grandpa works through them birds, though.

"Pay attention!" He says, "Gonna do a turkey." He wrastles it down, tries to steady the long gray neck on the elm block, half-choking it while its drumsticks kick his red-flannelled shirt.

"Keep still you bastard." It's the first time I've heard him curse. He's the kind of man curses with his face, not saying a word most the time. Turkey's no match for Grandpa. A blue-red slab of eyes and beak that was his head falls to the rocks with one sloppy hack. Sweat rolls down Grandpa's nose and he's breathing heavy. He hands me the axe.

"Your turn, boy."

I grab the handle. "Yep, it's heavy," he says. He sets up a block of firewood and grunts something that sounds like "Here."

My first swing I want to show Gramps I'm a man. I miss the wood and almost take off my big toe.

"Easy," he says, "boy. One chop down the middle all you need."

Second try isn't much better but I hit the wood. He nods and grabs a chicken by the neck.

"No Grandpa," I say, "I can't do it." I feel like a pussy. Grandpa says, "Just swing easy and straight. You hit my fingers, boy, your head's on the block next."

I line it up best I can, see the steel slice through feathers and veins to the stump. It must be a miracle cause I close my eyes and it falls right down the middle. It's cleaner'n I expected: blood leaks out sort of slow, pouring down over the limestone, black like chainsaw oil. It drips and rolls off the stump and mixes into Grandpa's turkey and chicken blood. Grandpa nods and grabs the carcass.

"Breakfast," he says.

Front porch is a real mess, with old tiles and tar-paper rolls all over. Uncle Jack pounds away up on the backside of the roof. Can't see him, just the dirty white old walls and a silver steel ladder. Wind's picking up from the north, so chicken duty's better than crawling around up there. Land around the house is pretty much open, except for the orchard. Grandpa's one of the few people left around here trying to grow. He's got a big enough field but the land here is rough for crops and the summer heat doesn't last enough to get a good harvest. The winter wheat and corn's fine, but not much else worth it. Most houses in the county got more trees right outside the house. All wide open here. The wind really whips through the fields and the patch of cement and limestone that runs between the house, red barn, apple orchard and Grandpa's work garage. Closest tree line's a quarter mile south. Goose bumps pop out the bare part of my arms, where I rolled the sleeves to keep off the blood. Didn't help much. There's blood all over me anyway and it's just colder, not having sleeves. Month ago, I was chest-deep in Lake Huron. Now, feels like snow's coming any day. Hard to believe, just two weeks ago we camped down at Search Bay. Caught lake trout big as my little brother Tommy from Jack's row boat. We could've lived a month out there on raspberries and trout, whittling driftwood around the campfire. No boots, no work, no chickens, just the warm sand on our feet and the shade of the spruce and pines to our backs. Just thinking about all that warm makes me feel even colder today.

I scrape my boots and step up to the screen door. It creaks when I reach in for the brass knob on the wood door with my slimy chicken fingers. Stepping in, I get a good whiff of my own stink before the smell of eggs and kielbasa fogs up the breezeway. My boots leave a blood trail on the green tile, so I wipe up the worst part with my sleeve. Grandma bangs around pots and pans in the kitchen. The sink runs full steam.

"Buck, that you? Bring me the garbage bags. Grab yourself a pop."

"Where?"

"Behind the wringer washer."

Everything's old in the back room, but it all works just fine. Grandma reminds me that every time I tease her about all these antiques. Says they made everything better way back then. The wringer washer, the iron, the oak laundry table—they all gotta be least as old as Grandma. I step out with bag and bottle. Walk fast past the brown wall to the kitchen, over a row of crusty work boots, gloves and tennis shoes. The kitchen's hot and messed with feathers, bags, boxes, newspaper and meat all around. Grandma's making raspberry jam when I give her the bags.

"My hands," she says, showing me a red jam mess. "Put 'em on the counter."

Grandpa sits down at the head of the table. Doesn't wash the blood off his hands, just starts eating. Grandma made me wash up. Take off my sweatshirt. Grandpa's sweating real good now and his brown overalls are red and purple-stained.

"Fetch me the bottle, woman." He winks at me and slaps Grandma's ass. She looks at me. Her mouth wants to say something, but it opens and closes and she don't. She pours from a fifth of Canadian Mist and slams the shot glass down on the chipped white formica in front of him. I wonder if she loves him. Even in their wedding picture she's got a sour face. Same look she makes now when Grandpa downs the shot and nods to my Coke.

"Good, boy, you brought the mix. First things first though. Afore the cocktails, we put some hair on your chest." He takes another shot, fills it up again and slides it over to me, like in a Western.

"Just a little eye opener."

"He's only twelve, Eddie." Grandma fixes his plate.

"Almost thirteen," I say.

"Wet your whistle. Atta boy. See that. Boy's got my blood in him. Takes after old Gramps."

"Gene and Mary gonna have your nuts in a wringer, old man," says Grandma.

"Brought Gene into this cruel world an bygod I'll take him out. Any man afraid of his own seed ain't much a man at all."

Both my eyes are open now and Grandpa fills the shot glass again.

The kitchen looks fuzzy. Everything moves slow motion—Grandpa, Grandma, the water from the sink. The clock ticks louder. Grandpa's snorts more angry. The chipped white ceramic on the counter drips blood and yellow chicken juice. Brown paper grocery bags full of feathers rock back and forth under air from the steel cage fan that moves side to side. Gramps bites his cracked lips, his face white-red and peeling. He shakes his head, snorts and pours another shot. I look at The *Last Supper* on the side wall, hoping he won't pour me another one, but he does. I drink it slower than the last one and start to gag before it's halfway down. Reminds me of shitty cough medicine. Grandma gives Gramps a love tap on the back of the head before she sits to his right and lights up a brown, filtered cigarette. Almost can't see her black curly hair under the red handkerchief, the same kind Gramps has hanging out his overalls. He plugs one side of his nose to shoot a string of snot out the other and wipes it on his flannel sleeve. Old country music plays on the radio till news comes on. Grandma takes another drag and puts out the cig in a Hills Brothers can.

"Take the gizzards and slop and whatnot to the burning barrel." She hands me a couple of Hefty bags and my arms shake when I try to keep 'em up above my waste. Grandma's stronger than she looks.

"Not so fast. Finish that there shot afore you go," says Gramps.

"The hell he will," says Grandma.

"Watch your mouth, woman. We don't need no lip from

you, do we boy." He winks at me while he slaps her ass again, a lot harder than last time.

It's a hell of a thing, being drunk. My arms and legs move but it don't feel like it's me. The steam coming out my mouth looks like Grandma's cigarette rings. I sing a whole verse of some dumb old country song before I notice Uncle Ray's smirking at me.

"I'll take those, Buck Owens," he says while I stand there looking stupid at him by the barrel. "The bags, fuckface. Damn, boy, thought you was s'posed to be the smart one. No common damn sense, just like your Aunt Virginia. Whole lotta good schoolin' did her. Damn waste a money, you ask me."

Veins stick out his neck. I try hard as I can to not laugh. I can't feel my fingers real good now. They sting they're so numb, but Ray pissed off is funny. Don't think I've ever seen old Ray happy. Not really. His words might as well fall on the concrete slab under the burning barrel with the spit shooting from his lips. I'm not listening to a damn thing. He slams the chicken bags into the rusted oil drum, and that's when it starts to pour. He pulls a Zippo out his shirt pocket.

"Go get that. The fucking can. 'Bout two gallons there?"

I slosh enough on the right knee of my jeans to light the barrel. Hand the can to Ray and he flips his Zippo.

"Get to the garage. Ain't gonna let up for a while."

A bottle cap clinks on the garage floor. Gramps hands Uncle Ray a Schlitz. Ray takes the bottle, looks at me and says, "See that frigerator? That's a fucking death trap."

"Don't make 'em like that anymore." Gramps clears his throat and spits on the floor.

"Like a fuckin' coffin you get stuck in one of them things. You're inside, door gets latched up, you're meat in the old icebox."

"Got that back in forty-nine," says Gramps. "Couple years after WWII."

"You were in World War II?" I look Gramps in the eyes.

"Don't dick around and stick one of your brothers or cousins in one of them fridges," says Uncle Ray. "You do that, they suffocate. Saw it on the TV. Monoxide poison it's called."

"Yep, first electric ice box we seen. Anniversary present for the old lady." Grandpa spits.

"Were you in the war?" I hate when older family don't listen.

"You been drinking, boy?" Ray stares me down.

"We might had an eye opener. Ain't that right, boy."

"Christ, Pa, he's twelve. Just a little shit. It'll be your ass when he goes home to Mary."

"Don't you blaspheme, boy. Asides, she's Irish. There ain't no other but that this boy's gonna be a drinker. Gets it from both sides, right boy." He spits and pulls the snuff can from his back pocket. "Boys want a pinch."

"You okay, Buck. Whatever you do, don't piss. Break the seal, you'll be pissing all day."

Soon as Ray says it, I feel like I gotta piss.

"Go sober up and help out the old lady," he tells me.

I follow the bloody trail from the garage back to the house, trying not to step on any heads or turkey slime. The rain stopped but there's puddles all down the driveway. Gramps and Uncle Ray fire up the grinder. I hear it hum in the garage. It can't be no later than noon, but the sky's darker. The air numbs my fingers, even though the sun peeks out from the gray. My right boot sinks past my ankle in mud. I really gotta piss now, so I squish away into the maze of apple trees off the west side of the house. I'm already pulling down the buttons on my jeans while I'm ducking into the trees. I can't get the last button, but the crotch heat feels good on my hands, so I stop, warm my fingers for a few seconds, then peel it out. Feels good letting out the poison. It's a real yellow color. I heard my mom tell the old man one time that dark piss means you're not drinking enough liquids. Sounds like bullshit to me. Gramps and I been drinking liquids all morning. I'm not playing with myself, but I keep my hands down by my dick for a little after I pull up my long johns, just to warm my hands some more. It feels good, all cozy down there, so I'm making strange noises when I feel a hand on my shoulder. Whoever it is got little girlie hands. I turn around, buttons undone, to give him hell.

"What you doing, you fucking faggot." I'm looking Father Pierre in his almighty face, but it's too late to stop the words.

"Lovely. I was looking for your grandmother, son."

"She's out here inside the kitchen." I always get nervous and talk stupid around people like Father Pierre, people that always sound smart when they talk. The whiskey shots sure aren't helping either.

"Profanity is a sin, my son. Consider your eternal soul. Break ties with those who would lead you on the path to damnation: 'But if you do evil, be afraid, for it does not bear the sword without purpose; it is the servant of God to inflict wrath on the evildoer.'"

"Aren't you s'posed to be a forgiver, priest?" He gives me a snot prick look but bites his tongue cause Grandma walks over from the front porch. She hands me another bag of chicken scraps.

"Morning, Father." Her face lights all up when she sees this fake. "Hey Buck, take this out and have 'em burn it." She stops, sighs and puts her hands on her hip. She pats me on the head and lights up a brown cigarette. They wait to talk till they know I can't hear.

Gramps is sharpening axes inside the garage. The garbage barrel is filled to the top so I leave the bag at the side of the garage. Ray must've walked out for a few minutes. I'm thinking he mighta gone home until he walks back in with a shotgun.

"Fuckin' squirrels," is all he says. Gramps is sweating and he stops to wipe off the axe blade. Then, he grabs another smaller one. He walks back to the chicken coop, double-fisted, and I gotta say it.

"Why two axes?"

"One's a axe. 'Nothers a maul."

"What you use 'em for?"

"One's for chickens, one's for bigger birds. Geese and turkeys and whatnot," says Uncle Ray, smirking, loading shells into the twelve gauge.

"Oh," I tell em, looking down. I'm kinda wondering which one is what but I suppose the bigger-handled one with all the extra metal must be the maul. I know what it means to maul. Learned it from a book I read in Mr. Miller's class. The bigger one would do a better job mauling, so I leave it at that.

"Hey, get out here, boy." Uncle Ray is shouting like nuts just outside the garage. "Take a shot at them squirrels. Already got me two of those bastards."

Grandpa nods out toward the door and Uncle Ray, so I go.

Gramps always says you can never get too much target practice. Never know when things are gonna get tough, but when they do, all you can really count on is family. "Nothing's thicker'n blood." That's what he always says. "The law won't protect you, the church won't save you and the government sure's hell don't love you." I've never heard him say he loved anybody either, but he's always talking about taking a bullet, even for the "least of his family." I know for a fact he'd do it too. All of us would.

Ray holds out the twelve gauge in firing position and helps steady it into my hands. I line up the bead with the closest target. The first shot almost knocks me down. Stings my shoulder from the kick. I'm used to a .410. Makes me off a little but I graze a fat little red squirrel enough to stun him. He just holds put there on the wet gravel. Uncle Ray walks over, picks him up by the hind end and smashes his head against a stump.

"No sense in wasting a shell. Tag 'nother one."

This time, I pop one in the neck hard enough to take it down for good. I hear the rest of the shot spray into the west wall of the barn.

"Nice shot. Go pick it up."

I walk past the turkey pen to the tool shed by the barn and bend down over the squirrel to see if it's moving. I grab it by the legs and look into its little black eyes, the head half-hanging from its body. The thing's heavy, limp and dead in my glove hand. Uncle Ray hands me his Buck knife.

"Here, keep the tail. Then bag 'em with them ones. I'll clean 'em and we'll fry 'em up for dinner tomorrow."

I'm still not sure just what I'm supposed to do with the squirrel tail but I put it in my coat pocket. That makes Ray smile. My head's starting to spin faster, kinda like when you have the flu.

"I think I'm gonna check on Gramma," is all I can spit out and I walk to the house again. Smart money says the main course for dinner tomorrow will be squirrel, or chicken. I don't mind the taste of squirrel so much—it's not a half bad meal when people know how to cook 'em right: with some butter, onion slices and season salt—just the shot's a problem. Nothing worse than eating rabbit, squirrel or partridge and getting a broke tooth with the shot. No way to really help it though, I guess, less you do all your small game hunting with a .22. Now that I'm thinking on it, not much fun when people don't know how to bone fish proper neither. How many times I almost choked on a fish bone? Grandma gets it right most the time, though. Best cook I know. Always takes extra time to dig out the fish bones and really gets in there to pull out the shot from the squirrels. She's hanging some socks and underwear on the clothesline when I'm walking all dizzy up to the house. She stops when Father Pierre says something and puts his hand on her shoulder. He moves it, kinda nervous, when they see me.

"You look like hell, son. What we gonna do with that old man, eh? Go lay down. You done enough for today." Father Pierre looks away. Fine with me, so I move straight through to the house, bloody boots and all. I wash up in the kitchen and then curl up on the old brown living room carpet. There's no pillow so I ball up my jacket. The warm air from the fireplace makes me tired fast. My stomach don't feel so bad, resting on my side.

I'm scared awake to glass breaking. Room's still real dizzy, so it takes a while to pull myself up. It's not that late, cause the sun is bright from the window by the couch. Grandma comes in, stands by the fireplace. Her right eye is purple and swolled up.

"Cops are coming. Damn nosy neighbors. Your Uncle Jack's with the old man, cleaning him up. When they ask, you tell 'em that you were playing ball with Jack and it went through the winda. You missed it. The winda smashed. That's what happened."

"What really happened?"

"Your Uncle Ray put the old man through the glass."

"Why? Ray wasn't even drinking."

"He was looking out for me, but like I told him, I don't need his help. Good sons mind their own damn business."

"What about your eye, Gramma?"

"Oh, this is nothing, you hear me. It was an accident. Hanging pants and slammed my head into the clothesline pole."

Father Pierre's black shirt and priest collar hang loose on a kitchen chair but he's nowhere around—strangest damn thing. There's bright red on that white collar. All I know now is I gotta see Gramps, so I move fast out the front door to the porch. He sits there where the porch meets driveway and rubs the back of his head. His white hair is stained red and he picks out glass, one little piece at a time. Hard to tell where the birds' blood ends and Gramp's starts, except the bright patches on his head. He looks me in the eyes, half teared up, half looking to kill. I know somebody's gotta do something. Gramps can't. Not right now. I run to the garage to look for Ray's twelve gauge but he must've took it. It's half a mile straight through the wood path to my house from the farm. I can run it two minutes, ten seconds. Uncle Jack timed me and says no one can run it faster than me, so I go for my .410. Only problem, today I'm not me, tripping in the grass dips of the wheat field and catching cedar roots all through the wet land trail that opens to a hill of spruce and birch.

Gramps will know what's next. I'm ready for everything, a bag of shells, a knife and my single shot at the ready. Only problem, I fail. Cops beat me to Grandma and Gramp's house by at least a minute. Everybody's gone. Gramps and Ray left chickens clucking free and they peck around in Grandma's garden, away from the mess. They already tore up the cabbage, now they're pecking at the potatoes and carrots. I pop one with the .410 and the rest go nuts. I keep walking down the trail to Uncle Ray's, shooting out the windows on all the junk cars to the side. I load, I lock, I ruin everything in my path: the '40 Woody, the '55 Buick, the blue '71 T-Bird, the white and orange Ford pick-up. The .410 kicks light on my shoulder till I'm numb. With my last shell, I hit a yellow deer crossing sign Uncle Jack stole and hung from a birch. The shot bounces back at me. It hits my chin, left ear, chest and falls on the sand around my boots. Hurts like hell, but there ain't no blood I can see. Then, I pull the knife. I stab everything worth stabbing, running fast as I can down the trail. Uncle Ray'll be pissed about the T-Bird. Bought some parts to fix it up for next summer. Might tell him tomorrow I saw the neighbor, Esther's kid, run through here with a gun.

I should run back home and get my pup tent—the one Dad brought back from Nam. Grab my pack and hike to Hessel. It's night, though, and I'm hungry—got no money and no more ammo for the .410. Mom and Dad aren't coming home today. Grandma's supposed to feed me, and my gut's about to give in. I walk past the field, the junk cars, the coop and make the turn north by the garage to Grandma and Grandpa's driveway. Most the chicken mess is gone, but there's still blood on the path to the front door. Even in the dark, anyone could see it. No noise comes from the house. The kitchen is quiet and dim, just the light over the sink on. The chicken parts are gone and the room has a strong Clorox smell. Gramp's bottle, just a couple shots left, sits at his place on the table. Grandma's back is turned. She reaches over to crank on the burner while she keeps washing dishes. Smells like there's stew in the pot.

"Might as well set down," she says, not turning around.

1994

Tracers hiss from both sides of the gravel road, and shrapnel impacts the front of our convoy. Then there's no more explosion, no screams, just the smell of canvas burning, the flickering lights from right and left—powder, ammonia and sparks in the thin, cool mountain air. The sun's almost down but there's still some red daylight over the rocky green hills. After the first mortar, we cleared out the trucks and took positions on both sides of the road. I'm on the left, downslope side. Guys on the right face a fifty-foot rock wall. No solid cover either way, just a few stones and bushes stick out from spotty grass. Best we can do is stay close to the ground, keep a low profile. I prop my chin on the butt of my M-16 and scan all around. The smell of the grass here isn't too different from the grass back home. I'm three months away from my ETS date and they're supposed to send me stateside by the end of the month to outprocess. Was hoping to get through my UN service time here without any problems. Then shit like this happens and time slows—every second passes like an hour. My heart's pounding so fast it feels like it's pushing my chest off the ground but I stay low. A mortar round impacts behind me at the top of the mountain. Then it gets real quiet till shots from the valley light up the hill behind us in a steady rhythmic hail. A gust of wind blows through from the north and the tracers slow to a stop.

It rained here last night and the dirt's still moist. Reminds me of when I was a kid and we used to spend most of our summers camping. Some days you'd wake up after a light rain and the ground was just wet enough to make it spongy, not muddy. Mom and Dad would always take time off from work in July, and we'd spend long weekends at Tahquamenon, Brevort, Search Bay or the Ontario provincial parks around Lake Superior. Dad cooked burgers and chicken on the grill while Mom baked potatoes and carrots in foil over the fire pit, all crowded in next to the blue steel camp pot they used to boil water for coffee. Johnny, me and little Tommy would look for berries in the woods—strawberries in June and blueberries and raspberries in July. Then we'd race on the beaches and take on the chill of lake water till we couldn't feel goosebumps. My legs tense when a grenade launches in from the valley—flies over our heads and explodes on the rock wall. Then the shots start up again and tracers light up the dusk with a bug zapper glow, rounds buzzing over our heads like giant fireflies.

Most of the summer, Mom and Dad had to work so we'd camp on our own—set up the tent in the backyard or the edge of Grandpa Eddie's field—spend our nights outside. In the daytime we'd bike out to Hessel and swim out at the cottage access or public beaches and pedal up to the field in time for little league games. On sunny days, a light breeze would blow through in the afternoon, no mosquitos, no ants, no horseflies, just the warm sun, buzzing of dragonflies and the grasshoppers' drumming. I might never hear that sound again. Sometimes, on the lazier days, I'd nap on a blanket, or just stretch out over the cut brome grass in the backyard. Bosnian grass has that same smell.

A grenade explodes a few hundred meters from the front of our convoy and the chopper blades hum from over the hills. There's another grenade, closer this time, in front of us on the downslope of the hill and the earth shakes my underside. Fragments clang against the steel frame of the truck that's behind me to the right and the hill vibrates with the aftershock. Small arms rounds pierce the air over my Kevlar helmet, so I pull myself closer to the ground, my right thumb and fingers gripping the bottom of my 16's handguard, my left hand clawing into the gravel, grass and dirt, pulling myself an inch at a time toward a tire-sized boulder, the only cover I see. More tracers sizzle over and the muscles in my head, neck and back twitch. My legs tingle. I want to crawl under the ground and hide but I keep moving forward to find cover, just the way I was trained. My head is sideways until I get to the rock. Then I peek around to scan for targets. After that last grenade, I'm not taking any chances. I straighten the barrel, my left hand steady on the bottom of the guard, until someone to my right yells out, "Hold your fire, dipshit. They ain't after us." Then our Apaches fly over, low to the ground, spotlights on and violent blades cutting into the gray air, the force pushing us further down into the ground. The hostiles from down in the valley retreat with their tracers, grenade launchers and mortar trucks. The steel birds follow the ambushers out until the hum softens to a faraway rhythm.

Never thought peacekeeping would be so damned confusing, but even conventional war isn't straightforward anymore. Here, everybody's trying to kill each other and we're left with the mess of policing it all. Bosnians, Croats, Serbs, Slovenes, blue hats from half the UN countries, who knows who else, all trying to sort out this mess. The shooting only lasted thirteen minutes. I kept track of time on the olive-green wristband watch I bought at the PX before we left for Europe. A half hour later, we're all clear, but it's a slow trip back cause the engineers need to sweep for mines on the road. It's standard operating procedure. Word is, one faction engaged another group on the hill above us and it was getting dark and everybody's trigger happy, so they hit our convoy too, not knowing we were UN. So his is how we'll end our day—stopping and starting the convoy through the mountain trails in 400 meter spurts. This will go on through the early morning till we get to our drop off point. Me, Wiggins, Robinson and Van Dorn were on this convoy to re-supply our checkpoint outpost and we were due back at midnight. This delay means no stop at Command, no shower, no beer for at least another two weeks, and, since I'm the ranking NCO of our group, I'll have to write a report to clarify that we weren't AWOL. The transportation Captain in charge of the convoy says three of our trucks were blown to shit but somehow there was zero troop casualties, just a few scratches. With the lack of trucks, a few dozen of us have to hoof it back. The front of PFC Wiggins' BDU pants are soaked. Nobody noticed until PFC Robinson shined the red light in his direction. He swears it's from taking cover in a puddle during the attack. Even if that's true, none of us will ever let him live it down.

For the seven of us, it's our first mail call in two weeks. We're lucky correspondence was on one of the trucks that didn't burn. Captain

Stubb gets a small box with chocolate chip cookies and a red pair of lacy velvet panties from his wife. Master Sergeant Perry has a box loaded with Pall Malls and Wrigley's Spearmint gum. Must be twelve cartons in there. PFC Wiggins gets a letter from his older brother. The return address says Alameda County Jail. Specialist Van Dorn gets a whole shitload of letters and boxes with rock candy, jerky and Grisham books. For PFC Robinson, there's one letter from his mom and another from his girl back in Palo Alto. I get just one envelope, from my brother Johnny. Sergeant Morgan gets a box of *Hustler* and *Penthouse* magazines with a few packs of Marlboros stuck in the open spaces on the sides.

"What's the letter from your old lady say, Captain?" Sergeant Perry asks. Stubb usually reads the dirty parts out loud and brags. Shows us pictures of Mrs. Stubb in bra and panties. Her name's Melissa and she was a football cheerleader at Georgia State. She always acts real proper and kind of snotty at the Christmas dinners. When we get back, me, Morgan and Perry won't see her so proper at the formal dinners. Everybody's sure she's cheating on him. Wiggins is always telling him, "No disrespect, Sir, but your wife is fine. You know Jody and his brother are hitting that while you over here."

Sergeant Perry slaps the Captain on his back and rough massages his neck with his thumbs and middle fingers.

"Not reading this one, Top. Yesterday was our anniversary," Stubb tells him. Sergeant Perry's just an acting First Sergeant, still waiting to make rank, not that it matters much here.

"Come on, Sir. Don't do us like that. Can't show us them panties and leave us all hard, wanting more," Wiggins says. PFC Wiggins is a white guy who acts black. PFC Thomas Robinson III is the only real black guy in our attachment, but he acts more white than Wiggins, so Wiggins calls Robinson Uncle Tom. Since they're both from the Bay area in California, they get along pretty good, but you can tell Robinson wants to jack Wiggins every time he calls him Uncle Tom.

"I'm definitely not reading this in front of Wiggins," Captain Stubb says. He'll steal these panties first chance he gets, make 'em all crusty."

"Come on now, Sir. You know I don't do you like that. Less

you leave 'em out in the open. No, that's a'ight, Sir. Morgan gonna read us a story from one of them *Hustler*."

"Stories in *Penthouse* are better," says Morgan, "but you wouldn't know that cause you can't read."

"Don't need to read 'em to gets what I want. You read that *Penthouse* and let me borrow that *Hustler*. All I need's ten minutes."

"Hell no Wiggins, not till I'm done with 'em. These are my girls."

"Man, you crazy," Wiggins says. Morgan walks off with his magazines to the stone building. Truth is, Morgan's a good soldier when duty calls, but we don't see him much otherwise.

"How 'bout you, Metzger? You get a letter from your girl?" Perry grabs my envelope, sees it's from my brother. "No fun here," he says. "Just family shit. How 'bout you Robinson?"

"Yeah, what you got Uncle Tom? Your girl send me some panties? Spray some perfume on that letter for me and shit?" Wiggins asks him.

"No, but your moms sent me her bra."

"It's all good, Uncle Tom. I ain't mad. I ain't mad. Yo moms sent me her panties and her garters last mail call. Her ass so big, them panties like a damn parachute, but that's some good loving."

Robinson pumps his fist at Wiggins but he calms and shakes his head when everybody laughs. Wiggins puts his hand on Robinson's shoulder.

"Easy brother," Wiggins says. "Looks like those veins gonna pop out your dome."

"You ain't my brother," Robinson tells him. Then he looks at all of us. "Wiggins too damned ugly to be my family."

"Your girl thinks I'm alright," Wiggins tells him. "When I get out next year, I'll take real good care of her till you ETS."

Everybody laughs again, then it quiets and we all go about our business, reading our letters and making coffee from the MRE packets. Perry gives us all a pack of Pall Malls. I'm not a smoker, but I take it anyway and light one up. It stops my hands from shaking. After I finish Johnny's letter, I go back to reading a book Katherine Beckett sent me before I left for Europe, *Light in August*. Just started reading it yesterday and didn't get too far into it, only about twenty pages. I'm hungry, tired and my legs tremble, even though I feel relaxed. It's hard to pay attention to the letters squirming on the page, so I re-read the same three paragraphs for a half hour. Then I just give up and light another cigarette.

1983

Great Uncle Liam finally drank himself to death last night. The older women always talk about how handsome he used to be, a real charmer—they all say he looked like an Irish Frank Sinatra. Ever since I can remember, he's been wrinkled with dark spots on his yellow skin. Even though he had a heavy frame, he always walked with his back straighter than anybody I know. He had the bright gray eyes of an elementary school kid and was always joking around. He'd give me and my brother Johnny a dollar every time we saw him and he always called us lady killers. You couldn't help but like the guy. That's probably why Grandma Clio's going to his funeral, even though she'll have to see all of her ex-family. Grandpa Mike won't be back from Texas. He's taking it hard, they say, drinking heavier than usual. It broke his heart cause Liam's more than a brother to him, he's his best friend, but Grandpa won't make it up. Says there's no point in coming now—it's too late.

Grandma Clio and Mom were supposed to go into town for the fall festival and look at crafts—wicker baskets, pumpkin candles, scarecrow art— like they always do this time of year. Instead, they're heading up to the Sault for the wake. Dad's plan for the weekend was to take care of the bear situation out by Grandpa Eddie's hunting cabin. Bear's been coming around eating deer bait. Grandpa Eddie baits for months before deer season starts to get the big bucks coming out by his cabin. He's up in Canada now, moose hunting with Lester Cronin. A big black bear started coming in and eating all the corn. Me, Jack, Johnny and Dad are going to take care of it this afternoon. Dad wants to kill it natural, with a recurve bow and arrow.

Grandma and Henry slept here last night. They were supposed to leave together after Grandma got back from the craft show with

Mom today, but with Uncle Liam dead, their plans might change. The counter and kitchen table are covered with beer cans and whiskey bottles from last night's poker game. Dad grabs the last two Old Milwaukees from the fridge and offers them up to Grandma and Henry. Grandma pops one open and Henry shakes his finger at Dad.

"No, Sir, no breakfast beer for me." He pours Scotch into half a cup of coffee.

Dad's frying up ham and eggs while Mom cleans the beer cans and ashtrays from the table, scrubbing down the beer and pizza spots with a hot green dishrag. Grandma swigs her Old Milwaukee and jams bread down into the toaster. Then she rubs her temples and cleans the sleep from her eyes with a wet napkin. Henry lights a cigarette and Johnny starts to cough when smoke rolls into the living room where he's watching Grizzly Adams on TV. Mom opens the kitchen window and the door to the front porch, then goes back to collecting cans and wiping down the table. A gust of cold air ruffles the living room curtains and gives me chills, then everything in the house calms.

"Gene, you going up to the wake?" Mom asks Dad.

"Thought we discussed this last night," he says. "Liam was a hell of guy, but I got too much to do this weekend. Besides, he's your kin. Don't need me up there."

Mom just gives him a look like he'll pay for it later when Grandma and Henry are gone.

"Would make it easier for Mom that way, not having to drive all the way back down here to drop me off," Mom tells him.

"How 'bout you, Mr. Taylor?" Grandma asks Henry.

"Woman, leave me out of this," Henry tells her. "These is your exes. You want to get involved, that's your problem, but don't go dragging me into it. I can stay and help Gene with whatever work he's got down here."

"Some gentleman you are," Grandma tells him. She laughs and finishes off her beer. "That's alright. You go help out Gene. Just don't get falling-down-stupid drunk again. Remember what happened last time."

"Yeah, Gene, why don't you take Henry out with you to get the bear," Mom says.

Dad catches Mom's attention while he shakes his head no.

"I don't know. It's a lot of walking," Dad says.

"Ah, hell, boy, you think the old man can't keep up with you? I'm in real good shape." Henry lights another cigarette.

"You could lend Henry some overalls and a rifle. All kinds of extra gear in the basement." Mom smiles at Dad while she gives him the devil eye.

"I don't want a be a burden. Y'all can just drop me off at home on the way up." Henry pours the last few drops of Scotch into his coffee and then he opens a bottle of Crown Royal to top it off.

"Ah hell, I was just messing around, Henry. Come on out with us," Dad says. "Let's see what kind of bear hunter you are."

"I'm the kind who gets good and drunk before I take that first step into the woods," Henry says. "The more I drink, the straighter I shoot. Damned cataracts."

"Well, we're on our way," says Dad. "Let's shoot some more of your Crown Royal before we head out. You know I don't get to drink that fancy shit unless you're around, Henry."

"Bear could've waited till tomorrow," Mom says.

"These women just don't make no sense," Henry tells Dad. He pours shots for Dad and himself. "Always squawking about something. Can't shut 'em up."

Grandma throws an ashtray at Henry from the kitchen to where he's sitting on the old recliner in the living room.

"Damn, woman, you nicked me," he tells her. Blood trickles slow from his left ear. "Least she didn't get my good side," he tells me. He laughs and wipes the blood away with his index finger.

"That's just a warning," Grandma says.

"We should probably make a casserole for Uncle Liam," Mom says.

"I guarantee Liam won't eat it," Henry tells her. Mom and Grandma ignore him and start looking for green beans and the cheese shredder.

"I'll bring you up some overalls and a thicker coat from the basement Henry, some gloves too, if you need 'em," Dad says. "Get you a rifle and some shells. Pick your poison—30.06?"

"Everything but the rifle, Gene. Got my .45 in the glove box. Plenty of ammo."

"Uncle Liam would've enjoyed hunting with you guys," Mom says. "He liked the big game."

Liam had all kinds of trophies in his game room. Everybody who's seen that room says it's better than that restaurant in downtown Sault, Antler's, the one with all the animal and fish taxidermy. Liam's room's even got lion and polar bear mounts. Might've even shot those himself. Him and Grandpa Mike were always on some adventure when the two of them were younger, hunting, fishing, drinking and womanizing—or like Grandpa Mike calls it, the good life.

"We need more ground beef for this casserole," Grandma says. "Should I pick up a case of Old Mil for these boys while I'm in town?"

"No," Mom says, "but if you don't, they'll get one anyway. Buck, you take good care of Johnny and don't let your Dad or Henry drive drunk. I'm taking Tommy with us—still too young for bear."

"We'll get him out there next year," Henry says. "Get him a shot at Old Ben."

"Not sure he'll be ready for that next year either," Mom says. She pulls Tommy in close to her, combs his hair to the left side and kisses his forehead.

"You keep carrying on that way, fussing around, that boy's testicles won't never drop," Henry says.

The beast moves downhill through the spruce and birch, splashing through spring holes, leaving twisted cedar branches and sunken tracks behind him. Dad follows the blood lines on the early patch of snow with his purple flashlight. There's grace in Dad's movement, the way the light never strays from the red splotches. Jack follows Dad, I follow Jack, Johnny follows me, all of us awkward in our steps. Dad runs, more wolf-like than human. There would be a beagle with us, but our dog Beck ran away from home. Dad says he likes it better this way anyway, man versus bear. The dog would make it too easy. Somewhere behind us is Colonel Henry. He gets along fine for 82, but can't keep pace with the rest of us, with the frantic chase. He might lag back now but he'll be there when we find the bear.

"Must be close by," Dad says. "Snorts are getting louder."

Dad holds up his left hand the way he must've done it in the Rangers and comes to a dead stop. Johnny runs into my back and half-falls between a rock and a spring. His pellet gun discharges, the ping crackling into the braches of a thick cedar.

"Quiet," Jack says. He's got his 30-30 at the ready. I've got the .22 pistol. Somewhere behind us, up the hill under the peeling birches is Henry with a silver-plated .45, the same one he carried for back-up in Ardennes and Normandy. Dad's got a Bowie knife in his right hand and a flashlight in his left. Our guns are just in case something goes wrong. Dad started the hunt without a gun and wants to finish it that way. He puts the blade of the Bowie between his teeth and lips and pulls something out of the muck. He turns back toward us and shines the light on gray metal: the nock, twisted crest and what's left of the fletching.

"He broke it off here," says Dad. "Might've slowed him."

"Think you got him good?" Jack asks.

Dad turns and scopes the opening with his flashlight. Before I notice the lantern behind me, there's a hand on my shoulder.

"You boys keep them weapons at the ready," says Henry.

"Don't even think about pulling the trigger less I tell you to," Dad says.

"Damn fool," says Henry. "Never give nature more odds than she already got."

Henry left Tennessee to fight in World War I. It was 1918 and the war was just about over. Henry was seventeen but looked older. After he got back from France, he stayed on for more: fifteen years enlisted, fifteen as an officer. Finally retired after the Battle of the Bulge. Henry's kind of a local hero, even though he's from Tennessee. I saw a letter he wrote to his mother in the town museum. He said, "I'm done with Europe. We're full-circle, back where we started in the first war, and there's not much left for me to do here. Let the Marines deal with the Japanese." Since then, he's been a gambler, a businessman and a dedicated alcoholic, usually all at the same time. He and Grandma Clio been together for thirty years. They live like a married couple but they're not. Henry's southern gentleman and scoundrel all rolled into one and has one of the sharpest minds of anybody I know. He's in better shape than most people half his age, thin and muscular, even though he chain smokes and drinks Scotch in the morning and rotgut at night. When he gets really trashed, he recites literature from memory. His favorites are Poe, Whitman and Faulkner. When we read Poe in my English class, I recited some of those poems from memory cause I heard Henry do it so many times. Mr. Miller couldn't believe it—thought I was reading from a cheat sheet. Henry can remember whole books and recites better the drunker he gets. Mr. Miller says booze makes you stupider—he wouldn't know what to make of old Henry.

A warm breeze blows in from the south when the cracking of the branches and twigs on the ground stops. I see Jack turn in the dark. He comes back to tell me and Johnny to stay quiet. I can't see Dad. Henry's still walking, but doesn't hardly make noise. There's thrashing in front of us and grunting. Jack signals us forward. The next grunt sends a chill through my neck. The bear is close. I didn't go the last time they tracked a bear. Mom said Johnny and me were too small. Part of me wishes I would have stayed back this time too, but it's a rush not knowing where the bear is. My pistol's at the ready.

When Henry recites Walt Whitman, it reminds me of Katherine Beckett, the prettiest, smartest girl in my class. Katherine said Whitman was gay when we read him for English. I told Henry what Katherine said and he told me, "Nonsense. America's second best poet was not a queer, boy. Who told you that? Even if it's true, why you go around telling the whole world about it—something not right with kids your age, Buck. Problem started with your daddy's generation."

Katherine's dad hunts too, but he usually flies off to some place like Alaska or Texas for his big game. Colonel Henry can read minds, I think. He knew I was thinking about a girl when we were back at the cabin earlier. He gave me all kinds of advice about women. He told me girls like guys who dress proper, wear collared shirts and ironed pants. I think he's behind the times. Even if he's right, how am I supposed to dress proper—like a gentleman—when I don't have the money to back it up like Henry does. Last night, Henry was real drunk back at the house and he told me to stand like a man, to walk with my back straight and my chest out. Slapped me real hard on the back to straighten me up. I'm sure he didn't mean to hit me hard as he did so I felt bad when Grandma Clio slapped him in the face and told him not to touch her grandson.

He was hurt, not so much from the slap. He just kept telling her, "Now damn it, you know I love these boys like they was my own." He must've said that ten times. Looked like he was gonna cry. But he didn't. He told me later that he hit me to straighten out my back cause ladies like a man with good posture.

We half-circle in on one side of the grunting in a wetland clearing. I step into a sink hole and feel the cold wet for the first time. Looks like everybody else already has wet boots and muddy pant cuffs except for Dad and probably the Colonel. He goes out of his way to step around the muck holes. Dad led the way running but somehow got past all the muck and water from the lowland springs and sinkholes. Dad's face is alert, his shoulder-length hair tied back neat in his red bandana, sweat on his forehead and cheeks shining in the yellow light of Jack's lantern. He readies his seven-inch Bowie. The bushes thrash and the bear whines and grunts ahead of us. Henry lifts the strap on his holster and Dad, with a wild smile, shakes his head no and signals his plan—runs the knife in front of his neck with a throat-slitting motion.

"Got-damn fool," Henry says in a loud enough whisper that Dad hears him. Dad's smiling face shines in the flashlight for a second, then he turns and crouches toward the grunts.

"Your old man's hell-bent on doing this without a gun," Jack tells me.

Can't see the bear, but it's close enough that the breathing's real loud. Dad takes slow steps toward the grunts and the bush until he disappears into the raspberry bushes and under the cedars. Henry pulls and cocks his .45. Jack kneels and aims the 30-30 toward the bent underbrush. I pull the .22 and Johnny mimics Uncle Jack, kneeling down next to him with his pellet gun. Henry sees Johnny's serious face in the lantern light and tells him, "That's right boy, you give that bear hell. Then, everything's quiet a good five minutes. The bear stopped snorting or I'm breathing so heavy I can't hear it anymore. Henry lights a cigarette with his left hand, .45 still cocked. Jack lowers the 30-30 and Johnny and me lower our guns too. A cold, wet splotch hits my cheek. Another falls on my head. Then there's a rustle in the bushes and we hear Dad yell out just before the chunking sound. The bear shrieks and then there's a healthy roar. The bear charges, first toward Jack and Johnny. Jack yells out,

"Gene, where you at?" In the second it takes for Dad to yell back, Jack doesn't pull the trigger and the bear changes direction—heads back to where it came from. Before it gets to the raspberry bushes, it jerks back toward me and Henry. The busted arrow in its shoulder shines for a second in Jack's lantern. Henry points, pulls, and there's a flash from his .45. The bear twists and claws toward us until it moves upright and Henry puts the second shot in his chest and drops him in his tracks.

Before Henry can holster his .45, the cold black sky lets loose, pelting us, mixing with the ground snow until it starts to slush and puddle up all around us. It's raining almost as hard as the storm we had back in July when me, Blake, Chelsea and Jay took Blake's dad's boat out to Mackinac Island. They had the Whaler docked in Hessel and Blake's dad told him we could take it out around the bay if Blake was careful. Jay got a hold of a six-pack of Heineken and Blake's mom must've left a half bottle of red wine on the boat. Chelsea doesn't drink beer so she sipped a little wine. After me, Jay and Blake finished the six, Blake said, "Fuck the bay. Let's go to Mackinac." We helped Chelsea finish off the wine on the way there. Even though she only had a couple drinks, she was goofier than the rest of us. Henry always says women don't have alcohol tolerance, except for Grandma. It's only about a fifteen minute boat ride from Hessel to Mackinac Island, so we didn't think there'd be a problem. When we got there, we tied up at the public dock and went looking for our friend George. He lives on the island in the summer cause his family owns a burger place. He always told us he could get us a free meal if we came out to the island. Never did find George but we ended-up eating there anyway, paying double what you'd pay for a burger on the mainland. I had to borrow three dollars from Chelsea to pay for mine. Blake said I was lucky Chelsea lent it to me cause he wouldn't. Said he'd laugh while my poor ass washed dishes to pay for the burger. Sometimes I'm not sure why he's my friend. All we got in common is we play baseball and basketball together and my good friends are his good friends. After lunch, we walked around Huron Street for a while till Chelsea couldn't stand the horse manure smell anymore. Blake wanted to see the fort so we headed up the bluff past the crowd in the park. There was a stage set up, so we figured something must be going on. We got about halfway up and it just started pour out of nowhere. It was about eighty degrees and sunny and the clouds and the wind just came in—the temperature must've dropped to about sixty by the time we ran back to the dock. We should've waited out the rain but Blake didn't want to get caught on the island too long. Didn't realize how late it was and he knew his dad would worry when he saw the rain and expect us back. Blake couldn't see much with all the wind and rain. The sky was dark as dusk and Blake's boat had a light out. Took us more than two hours to get back, the way the rain came down. Blake's old man left early from work and he was waiting for us by the dock when we got back to Hessel. Said he was close to calling the county boat cops. Blake was crying and his Dad was pissed, but he didn't get the ass-whooping I would've expected—just a talk about how he disappointed his parents, then his old man let him off easy and told Blake he was happy that everybody was okay. My ass sure would've been tanned.

The rain tonight started out like that rain from last summer, but it's a lot colder. It stopped after just a few minutes but it was enough to melt some of the snow without ruining the tracking. There's still blood everywhere in the flashlight's glow. The bear is a dark red-stained pile of black on the low edge of the clearing. Dad's green shirt is blood and rain soaked and there's a claw mark on his left sleeve.

"You okay?" Jack asks him.

"Not too deep," Dad tells him. "Just a little scrape."

Henry's takes a knee at the bear's head side. He pulls Dad's knife from the pile.

"Missed his heart by a couple inches," Henry says.

"Your shot was dead on, Colonel," Jack says.

"He's a good 375," says Dad. He wipes his face with his bloody sleeve. His pants are ripped and his neck and chin are bloodied and mud-caked.

"Maybe 400," Jack says.

"Now, the fun part," Henry says. "I finished the son-of-a-bitch off—y'all can haul it back."

Even with four of us pushing and pulling, moving the bear over the ruts, branches and muck takes a long time, kind of like hauling a 400 pound sack of sand—nothing real solid to grab on to except for the legs—and when you pull real hard, it almost feels like they might come right off the body. There's a lot of cursing and stopping to get a better hold. Dad and Jack are some of the toughest guys I know and the bear carcass is really kicking their asses. We finally get Dad pulling from the front, walking backwards, and Jack holding the hind legs. Johnny and me try to prop it up from the middle but there's even less there to grab on to and the trek is slow. Even with our new plan we got to stop every few minutes so Dad and Jack can rest and re-grip. I thought hauling deer was bad, but bear is almost impossible. Johnny and I aren't even doing much pulling and my arms are sore. Henry was walking ahead with the flashlight, but he disappeared a while ago. Probably back to the cabin by now. Johnny has to hold the other light now and I help Jack carry from the back. Dad never looks behind him, but somehow he doesn't run into anything. He really knows these woods.

The last person in the family to kill a black bear was Grandpa Eddie. That was years back, before even Uncle Jack was born. His bear was just as big as the one Dad got, maybe bigger. Kept coming around, stealing apples, so Gramps had to take him out. Only problem, he left the carcass right in the open when he went to get his camera and a DNR pulled up, old Wade Hamilton. By the time Gramps got back out, Wade was writing up a poaching ticket. Gramps told him to stop it and when Wade didn't, he pulled out his Zippo and lit up the ticket pad. They say it flamed up so fast old Wade damn near burned his fingers. Wade told Gramps he was going back to his truck for another ticket book. Told Gramps he was getting two tickets. Gramps lit his pipe and pocketed his Zippo. Pulled his coat back like an old west gunslinger and tapped the wooden handle of his .38 with his middle and index fingers. "You ain't writing me no ticket on my own property, Susie," he told Wade. Uncle Ray said old Wade's right hand started to tremble and he stuttered when he told Grandpa, "Mr. Metzger, I'm going for back-up and we're taking you in." Grandpa told him, "You or any other game warden ever set foot on my property again, and I swear to Christ Almighty, I'll bury you where you stand." Nobody ever saw Wade Hamilton after that. Uncle Ray said he got a transfer over to Negaunee.

Before we're even back at the hunting camp, Dad and Henry are at it again. Last week, Henry started in on how all Vietnam vets are pussies. Dad ignored him and that just pissed Henry off. Said it must be true if Dad didn't defend himself. Dad told Henry he's lucky he respects old people or he'd knock his ass down a notch. Henry took a swing at him from the table. We think the punch started out a joke but it's always hard to tell with the Colonel. Henry was so drunk he fell down from the table and cursed everybody out when they started laughing. Telling everybody he wanted to take it outside when he was lying down on the floor. This time they're fighting about the best way to skin the bear. First Henry was on Dad's case cause we didn't put a tarp under the bear when we hauled it in. Says we might've ruined the hide. Dad says it don't matter and that it wasn't worth walking back to the cabin for because it wouldn't have made much of a difference in the haul. Then he told me and Jack that Henry doesn't know nothing about bears just loud enough for Henry to hear him. Henry told Jack he knows all about hides. Says he's been tanning buckskin and bearskin rugs since he was a kid. Dad just hands over the Bowie knife to Henry and says, "Show us how it's done, old-timer." Dad and Jack roll the bear on its backside and Henry goes for the bottom of the neck like he's some kind of backwoods surgeon. He sets down the cane and his left hand shakes a little when he kneels in for a better cut, but his right hand is steady with the knife.

"Jack, you see what I see?" Dad asks. "Could it be a sow?"

"Ain't no boar, less he was castrated," says Jack.

"Johnny, Buck. Go get the big cooler, then find some firewood. Get that campfire started," Dad says.

There's no electricity at Grandpa Eddie's hunting cabin, no running water and no telephone. It would've been a three-mile sprint to the next house for a phone if the bear would've got to one of us. A wood stove keeps the place warm and kerosene lamps light the kitchen and card table. Water comes from the cast iron pump by the wash basin. Dad installed it for Grandpa inside the cabin to keep the pipes from freezing. For the third straight day, Dad, Johnny and me are gonna eat Dad's venison chili. Dad brought out the leftovers in a gallon ice cream bucket—figured we might be late and have to spend the night. Jack warms up the chili in an old camp pot over the gas burner and heats a frozen loaf of Grandma's oat bread over the woodstove. Henry scrubs the blood off his hands with a white rag. He wrings the red drops from the cloth over the wash basin, then pulls a fifth of Glenlivet from his long black coat and slams it down on the table. Dad pulls a pint of Jim Beam from the back right pocket his green overalls and sets it next to the Glenlivet. Then he passes out white styrofoam coffee cups to everybody and says, "Let's drink to the bear."

"Even me and Johnny?" I ask him.

"It's a special occasion," he says.

"Break out the cards," Jack says.

"What's the game?" Henry asks Dad.

"Euchre," he says. "You and me against Buck and Jack. Old guys versus the young'ns."

"Shit, you don't know what old is," says Henry. "I got hemorrhoids older than you."

"Ace no face is a misdeal. Dime a point."

Last July I went camping for a week out by Brevort Lake with Jay and Ronnie. Jay told his parents he was going with my family. I told Mom I was going with Jay's family. Ronnie's parents don't give a shit. We pitched tents and cooked cans of barbecue beans over the open fire pit. Grilled rainbow trout and sunfish in tin foil over the flames.

When we ran out of water, we walked up the hill to the springs on the north side of the lake. Jay's grandpa told him that his family's been using that spring since before the French came. We stopped and picked blueberries on the way back until the mosquitos got so bad in the low areas we couldn't take anymore. That's when Jay talked us into doing a vision quest, except we just spent one night out in the woods alone, not even a mile from the campsite, out in the hardwoods. Ronnie stayed in the tent to watch our stuff cause he already found his spirit animal with his uncle: a gray fox. I saw a squirrel with a bear in my dream. Jay told Ronnie that he saw a blue jay, then a trout, then a coyote. Ronnie told him he had to keep the blue jay, cause that's what he saw first. I just told them about the bear so I wouldn't get stuck with the squirrel. Jay said it wasn't fair—that I cheated. I told him it's not my fault he got stuck with a pussy animal and I didn't. Ronnie said the blue jay was a good animal too—just that it has some female qualities. Every time I see Jay alone at school he tells me I'm not a bear. He should be the bear because he's the biggest guy in our class. I just tell him, "Whatever you say, blue Jay," and he gets all pissed off. Jay's a good dude. He's always my Euchre partner when we play on the bus for baseball road trips. He's not as good at Euchre as Uncle Jack though.

For a decorated war hero, Henry sure is a cheating son-of-a-bitch when it comes to cards. Me and Jack have a four point lead and he's been looking at the three cards in the discard all game long. He's table-talking with the old man and trying to look at Jack's hand every time Jack reaches for the bottle to pour a shot.

"Whiskey's about dry," Dad says. "Johnny, go get that case of Old Milwaukee from the porch."

"When do I get to play cards?" Johnny asks him.

"Next game you can play for me," Jack says, "if you get me a bowl of that chili and a couple beers."

Jack calls a loner in diamonds. Wipes out Henry and the old man. It's overkill since we only really needed one point to win. That's three games straight we took from Dad and Henry. Even after Jack won the point with both Bauers and the ace of diamonds, he made everybody play it all out. Henry threw his jack of clubs at Jack in the last hand and it landed in his chili.

"I'm tired of these damned Yankee games," Henry says. "How about some five-card stud?"

"Long as I can play," Johnny says.

"Get the poker deck," Henry says. "I'll deal. Just need to freshen up."

He takes Dad's purple construction flashlight and a crusty roll of yellow toilet paper with him to the outhouse. When the cabin door closes, Dad tells me to keep an eye on Henry from the window. Henry walks slow and sways to the side every few steps like he's doing a strange sort of drunk dance. The flashlight shines in crooked patterns on the ground and evergreens. Henry almost wipes out at the end of his walk but he stays up with the help of the outhouse door.

Last Christmas, right in front of the whole family at dinner, Henry told us a story about how his best friend, Sergeant Dixon, died from a gut shot. They grew up together in Tennessee, even enlisted together. Henry said he watched him die for hours. Tried to stop the bleeding but there was nothing he could do. First, Henry looked like he was gonna cry when he told the story, then he started laughing till he fell out of his chair. Then he said, "That Dixon was a bleeder—even when we were growing up—yessir." Then he blanked out for the rest of dinner with this real serious look on his face the whole time. Great Uncle Liam was there, right at the end of dinner. Stopped by for dessert and a Thanksgiving toast with his fifth of Old Dublin. He put his arm around Henry and toasted him—called him a war hero—really lightened the mood. Made everybody except Henry comfortable again.

Dad says there's three kinds of veterans. There's the loud mouth braggarts who do nothing but talk about the war and tell stories that can't be true. They're mostly liars and cowards who panic the first sound of gunfire.

There's the quiet type who do their duty but don't say much. These are both the regular guys or the guys you have to watch out for. What they have in common is they all have a conscience.

Once in a while you run into a guy like Henry, Dad says. These people stump you cause they don't fit into the first two categories. Someone like Henry is matter-of-fact when he talks, you have to believe he's telling the truth, even when it sounds like bullshit. Grandma says most of what he says, the important details, is documented cause he had writers following his unit around for most of World War II.

Henry comes back from the outhouse shaking.

"I'll never get used to this cold," he says. "Back in Tennessee, dips down into the twenties and people put on two winter coats. Nobody goes outside without good reason, I'll tell you. Cold as a steel chastity belt in Norway out there, boys." Since he retired from the Army, Henry's lived most his life in Michigan, but he's still got a thick drawl and he's always talking about how bad the weather is.

"What's a chastity belt?" Johnny asks Dad, then looks around at the rest of us.

"Get used to it, Henry. Ain't that cold and it sure as hell's not getting any warmer today," Dad says.

"How about another round of Euchre?" Jack looks around the table.

"You know what's a real game," Henry says, "Roulette."

"Sure, break out the Roulette wheel, old man, and we'll play a round," Dad says.

"Yessir, that's a beautiful game. Sublime as war, right Gene," Henry says.

"If you say so Colonel," Dad says. "Deal the cards Jack."

"Deal me out," Henry says. "I feel those chili gasses coming on again. Where's your flashlight?"

"Again," Johnny asks him?

"Don't know what your old man puts in that stew, boy, but it does something right awful to my innards."

Dad takes Grandpa's yellow battery radio from on top of the pantry and feels for the power switch in the dim green light. A wind gust slams the cabin door shut while Henry's hand still holds the knob.

"Got some juice left," Dad says when the radio squeaks and big band music comes on. I don't know too much about Grandma and Grandpa's generation, but I know this song. It's Artie Shaw, one of their favorite records, just don't know the name of the song. Dad turns the knob to find something else and he hits an old country station, then a polka station, nothing else. Funny cause these are the only types of music Grandpa Eddie listens to. Dad moves the dial back and forth a few times and almost picks up a rock station, but it fades in and squawks out every few seconds, so he settles for the polka station.

"Let's see what old Henry says about this when he gets back," Dad says.

"Shit, he's too deaf to hear music," Jack says. Then there's crashing sound, metal on metal. Then another loud thud, and we hear Henry cursing, almost in time with the polka's tuba. Dad runs to the window.

"What is it?" Jack asks.

Dad laughs and tells him, "Henry took a spill. Knocked over the old man's fish shack on the way down." Grandpa Eddie's ice fishing shanty doubles as a mobile deer blind—it's got wheels for land and metal runners for the ice. Grandpa keeps it out by his cabin till the lakes freeze over and hauls it out to Government Bay with his busted-up Polaris. We all get our boots on without lacing up and run out to Henry.

"Who put this gotdamned contraption right smack on the road to the shitter?" Henry yells out when he sees us. The shanty was a good three yards off the path to the outhouse, but Henry walks in wider ovals the more whiskey he drinks.

"I'm coming Henry," Dad says. He turns to wink at the rest of us. "Told my old man to move that fucking death trap out of the way."

"Yeah, buddy. That shack fall the other way and I'm a dead man."

Dad holds out his arm to Henry but he pushes it away. "I ain't that old," Henry says. "Can still stand up myself." He tries to stand and slips half-way up, catches himself on his right elbow. Dad grabs the back of Henry's coat to steady him the second time he tries to get up. Henry brushes off the snow and ice from his pants and from under the green, winter army coat liner he borrowed from Dad.

Then, Henry quotes a poem I've never heard before, "Time drops in decay, like a candle burnt out, and the mountains and woods have their day, have their day."

"That's real pretty, Henry," Dad says. "Let's get inside and you can sing us some more."

"It ain't no song, you damned hippie delinquent," Henry says. He laughs and Dad laughs. Then he puts his head down and mumbles something to himself. Then he says, real clear, "Be scared. You can't help that. But don't be afraid."

"What's that supposed to mean, Colonel?" Dad asks him.

"Don't ask me," he says. "That's Mr. Faulkner."

Dad puts his left arm under Henry's arm and shoulder, props him up, and carries him into the cabin.

Henry was out cold for a half hour, then he hit his second wind. Woke up and noticed the polka music. I figured it would be safe to use the outhouse now, but it smells like a roadside rest stop in the dead heat of August. Even with the cold and an hour of fresh air, I need to bury my nose in my sweatshirt collar. There's a roll of toilet paper in a Folgers can and a box of .410 shells on the seat. Nobody left anything to read, so I read the box of shells. Grandpa usually keeps magazines out here but they're all gone now. There's a sound right outside the outhouse, like hound dogs with asthma. I pull up my overalls and unlatch the wooden door. I shine a light out toward the bear hide. Something's moving—three bear cubs are sniffing around. Kind of scares me at first, seeing the bears, but they're just cubs, so I walk backwards to the cabin, keeping my eyes on 'em the whole time, watching out for a bigger bear, with a chill down my back.

"You guys gotta see this," I say when I get to the door. "More bears out there."

Henry draws his .45 and moves faster than the rest of them to the cabin door. He walks toward the closest cub and when he's a little more than arm's length away, he points the barrel at the cub's nose and pulls the trigger. The cub drops and the others squeal. One lopes toward Henry and he puts one shot in the right shoulder and another in his neck. Henry ignores that one, even though it's still breathing, and looks to the last cub. Uncle Jack puts a shot between the wounded cub's eyes and puts it out of its misery. He's in his long johns and socked feet. He was looking for his boots but ran out of the cabin when he heard the shots. He looks at Henry and then me. Just shakes his head.

"Might give a guy some warning before you start popping off the hand cannon."

The last cub stands on its hind legs and Henry points and clicks from twenty feet, but the pistol misfires.

"Buck, shoot that sombitch," Henry yells at me. He tries to fix the jam but his hand shakes. "Damned arthritis," he says. "What are you waiting for, boy?"

I draw my .22, pull back the slide and click off the safety. Not sure a .22 can take down a bear cub, something I didn't think of earlier when we were chasing down the sow. It's gonna take one hell of a shot. Besides, I don't want to shoot a cub.

"Hold on there," Dad says. "What's going on here?" He's in his long johns too but he took the time to lace his boots up.

"Take down that bear," Henry tells me.

"Look at this mess," Dad says. He grabs the pistol out of my hand. "Let it go."

"It's good as dead without the sow," Jack says.

"No, we can take it up to the petting zoo in Naubinway. Might even give us a couple hundred for it," Dad says.

The cub walks toward Henry and we all step back.

"Just shoot the cocksucker," Henry says.

"Ain't gonna get no money without the DNR involved," Jack says. "They'll be asking all kinds of questions about where we got it. Too much hassle, Gene."

Dad gives Henry a pissed off look.

"Sure there's no other sow around?" He makes a quick walk around the edges of the clearing to scope out the woods around us and yells to Johnny, "Get the shotgun."

Johnny hands him the twelve gauge and runs scared back to the cabin. Dad lines up the cub with the shotgun bead, pumps it, then lowers the barrel. He takes his finger out from the trigger guard and hands the twelve gauge to Henry.

"Finish what you started," Dad tells him.

Henry gives me the shotgun. "Your turn," he says.

Everybody's watching me. The rain stopped and it's colder now. Everybody's tired. Dad signals for me to give him the shotgun. Henry shakes his fist at Dad and tells him to back away, then he grabs my arm and points the twelve gauge toward the cub. I look up to him and he says, "Cub's gonna die. Might as well be you, Son."

I brace the stock against my shoulder, line it up and squeeze. The recoil burns my shoulder. I eject the shell and pump another one into the chamber.

"That's my boy," Henry tells me. "Yeah buddy, that's how you put down a bear."

Henry was the first one up this morning. I caught him looking out the window at the snow coming down. We were up until five in the morning cleaning and skinning the cubs. We put all the good meat in Hefty bags and locked it up in Grandpa Eddie's fish shanty with the sow meat. The slops we put in burlap sacks and hoisted up around a maple branch to keep the coyotes from getting at it. We brought the hides into the cabin to dry, so it smells like the landfill out on State Avenue. When they had me take out the last cub, it took two shots, but I gave it a third, just to be safe. Henry was the first one to get to work, cleaning up the mess. Grabbed the first cub by the ears and pulled it out to the butcher stump. Dad joined him and then we all worked together to finish it up, Johnny and me doing most the running back and forth.

When Henry saw I was awake, he poured himself a shot and we sat at the table and talked. He told me about a lady he fell in love with when he first moved to Detroit. Then he talked about what it was like in the 20s, the Depression and earlier, when he was a kid. He said his favorite decade was the forties cause he finally had enough money to have fun, even with World War II going on. Henry and me both held our morning piss for about an hour but we finally gave in and put our boots on—stepped out by the woodpile, into the crisp morning breeze. Then Dad woke up a while ago. Unzipped his sleeping bag and marched right out into the snow, barefoot in his long johns, and pissed off the side of the porch. He brought in a few slabs of bear meat and now he's making bear bacon and eggs. The eggs are frozen, so he put a pot of water on the gas burner to boil.

"Have to make a couple trips out to the truck with all the meat," Dad says. "Wonder if the ladies got caught in that sleet last night."

"Isn't that something, that Liam," Henry says. He pours himself a shot from what's left at the bottom of the Scotch bottle. "Good thirty years younger than me. Don't smoke as much as I do, no real health problems and he's gone one day to the next. I'm still here kicking around, son-of-a-bitch I am. How you figure that?"

"Problem with a guy like you, Henry, the devil don't know what to do with you."

Henry smiles, lights a cigarette and sips his Scotch. "Gene, if you got a haircut I just might adopt you, boy."

1994

It's eight o'clock and I'm the last man in the library. That flabby old hag who runs the place, black cord on her red-framed glasses, shelves trashy romance paperbacks. The younger librarian works the front desk. The skinny old reference librarian exhales loud when she slams her stack of books on the counter, staring me down the whole time. The girl at the desk is about my age. Her name tag says "Martha." She's thin but wears baggy, hipster, Salvation Army clothes, her long, light-brown hair in a ponytail. Martha's green eyes dance when she sees me. She's awkward sexy. Even though she smiles while she stamps the back cover of the green, hardcover book, she takes her cue from the older women.

"We're closing," she says. "You won't be able to check out anything else today, I'm afraid."

"Maybe I'll see you tomorrow then," I tell her. Her smile disappears.

"No, tomorrow I have the day off."

She'll go home to a warm bed. For me, it's back to the street. Been sleeping in my car for a week now. Freezing rain sprays down, dense as beer vomit on the faded blue marble steps of the library. I almost slip coming out the door so I stop and lean against a stone column by the entry. I'd wait out the rain here but the hags might call the cops, so I step down toward the stone lions at the bottom of the steps. I walked here all the way from where I parked on Easterday Avenue. It's at least a good mile from the library.

I'm hungry and need a drink. Six dollars and twenty-three cents in my pocket. There's two hundred and fifty more locked in the glove compartment of my Buick, next to my .44 pistol. No ammo left in the clip though. Popped off every last round I had shooting lawn gnomes on the way to the Sault. That was the night Stacey dumped me. That two-fifty's got to last a while till I figure things out. With the cash in my pocket, I'll get a buzz and fill my stomach.

I was living with my parents. It's been three months now since I got discharged from active duty. Last week, the old man told me to get the hell out. Said that when he was my age he was married and living on his own for four years. I've been working on the islands, trying to save for college next fall. Not like I was freeloading. I tried to tell the old man that it would take me longer to start school if I had to rent a place, even if I could find a roommate. Told him I would pay him back later. He wasn't buying it. When I calm my nerves, I'll get a new job here in the Sault. Or maybe I'll meet up with my cousin Ryan in Dearborn.

It's been cold, sleeping in the Buick. The first night I left it running with the heat on. Listened to the same Radiohead cassette most the night. Woke up in a sweat. Then I turned the engine off and woke up freezing. It's been like this for a week now. First night, a cop rapped on the windshield and told me to go home. I just parked down another street where the houses are run-down—mostly college kids live there. Nobody's messed with me since.

Walking back to the Buick last night, a guy followed me past St. Mary's Cathedral. He was a strange dude, probably in his 40's, but he walked with a limp, like a man twice his age. I call him Uncle Pervie cause he looks like a child molester. That's when I drove to a new spot on Easterday. I try not to drive anywhere if I don't need to. Can't waste gas.

When I get to the intersection at Ashmun, Uncle Pervie's there. I see him good now. He's missing his left hand and he's got a red, v-shaped scar on his left cheek. The way he walks, he must sniff glue or something. I try to ignore him but he gets in my face.

"Hey, you," he says. "Give me a dollar."

"Don't have a dollar," I say. Pervie's normal-sized, but gimpy. There's a nervous half-smile on his pale face.

"Hey, Metzger. I've seen you before."

"How you know me?" I ask him.

"I wasn't always like this you know." His voice is high-pitched for a man his size.

"How were you then?" I ask him.

"I'm gonna fuck up every last one of you," he tells me. He tries to grab my throat with his right hand. "Die Metzger!"

I smack his chin with the hardcover copy of *Dubliners* I borrowed from the library. The complete works of Poe that I keep in my trunk might've been better, but Joyce does the job. Pervie falls back. I run until I'm three blocks ahead of him, past the clock on the three-story bank. It's dark and nobody else is out in the streets. I look back and Uncle Pervie's still cussing me out from outside the shoe store. I go another block. He turns and walks back toward the Locks, swinging his left arm around in the damp air. I duck in to the entryway of the Woolworth store to catch my breath and get out of the wind. There's chipboard where the windows used to be and a "For Sale" sign on the door.

I'll have to park somewhere else tonight, maybe out by the Neebish ferry docks.

First things first, though. I double back and hit the liquor store on Portage.

Drunk math dictates that two bottles of malt liquor leaves enough for four cheeseburgers. I know the blonde at the register. Partied with her in high school. Says she's a Nursing student now. From good stock, no doubt. Tattooed white trash with money. Don't know much about her family but I know she didn't dress like that back in high school. Still, she's too classy for malt liquor, so I opt for a six of Budweiser.

She takes her break and we sneak a couple in the parking lot out by the Palace Saloon. She keeps teasing me and touching my arm. I know she'd go anywhere with me tonight. Bet she'd cut out of work if I say the word. She's smart enough, easy on the eyes and dresses tight. She leans into me, like she's gonna kiss me, then snatches my book.

"I'm into Irish history, literature," I say. She looks at me funny. Can't tell if I'm serious.

"I get off at 11:00. We should meet up at Maloney's," she says.

Half a six barely numbs the cold and she wants more. Waits for my move. There is none. All I got is the Buick and its weeklong sweat stench, a backseat full of army duffels, books, empty bottles, sweat-socks and burger wrappers.

"Maloney's," I say. "11:00."

"Sarah. Back to work," a fat, greasy, bald man says from out the liquor store window. Sarah runs back across the street in her thin brown bomber jacket. Turns to smile before the door slams and the bells clang on glass and steel.

There's another party store before the bridge. Got enough left for two burgers or a Mickey's. Burgers are a mile away. The wind from Lake Superior picks up. Looks like more rain coming from the north.

Things could get better. Just need a plan. I switch the Mickey's from hand to hand to keep my fingers from freezing. Gets even colder on the bridge at Ashmun Street. Uncle Pervie must've followed me here. When I'm halfway across, he picks up his speed. Uncle Pervie wants me at the icy bottom, screaming in canal water. If I just run, Pervie could never catch me, but I lost my copy of *Dubliners*. Either Sarah has it, or I dropped it on my way to the bridge. I was reading a story called "An Encounter" when the library closed. Didn't get to finish it.

"You don't fucking know me," I yell back to Pervie, my words echoing over the dark waters of the canal.

Two weeks ago tonight, I broke down the Cronins' front door—kicked it in with my combat boot. The Cronin farm is the same place it's been for the past fifty years, down an old dirt road off of Blindline. I turned off my headlights, put the Buick in neutral and rolled into their driveway. Colonel Henry had an 1860 Colt Army that his Grandpa used in a bar fight. He won. Never used that revolver again. Henry brought it north with him when he came up from Tennessee. Kept it wrapped in blue silk in his second desk drawer. When I was twelve, Grandpa Mike gave me the Magnum. I showed the Magnum off to Grandma and Henry. Henry pulled the revolver out of the drawer and said, "Here's one to match it." He gave me the history a couple years later and told me that if I ever needed to take care of business, the revolver was better than the Magnum cause nobody would ever trace it back to me. He said this in front of Mom and she kicked his ass out the house that night. Never used that Colt before on anything but beer bottles out in the field. I'd practice drawing it like an old west gunslinger, but never fired it in anger. Thought about using it that night on Lester Cronin, but it stayed in my trunk. Had a better plan for him—didn't deserve to go that easy.

The aluminum screen door to Cronins' farmhouse was locked, but the glass cover was broken so I just ripped open the screen with my Buck knife. Then I opened the ash door with one kick. I expected someone to hear it and meet me in their sitting room. Nothing but boots, coats and wicker chairs. Then I called out Lester. Told the son-of-a-bitch coward to come get what he deserved. I figured they might call the cops, but by the time County got there, it would be too late. One of us would be down. I cursed him out a good ten minutes while I walked through every room looking for him. Then the bathroom light clicked on behind me and the Buck knife fell out of my cargo pocket. Agnes Cronin was there in a flannel night gown. She wasn't scared at all, just asked me if I was Eddie Metzger's boy. "Grandson," I told her. "Handsome man, your father," she said. That's when I remembered she wasn't right. More than a year back, in August, we were training at JRTC in Louisiana and I got a letter from Johnny. He told me Lester Cronin died and Agnes started going batshit crazy after the funeral. How could I be so fucked-up that I forgot Lester was dead? Ever since Bosnia, my memory's been a little out of whack and sometimes I can't even remember what year it is. I could tell by Agnes' eyes that she was full-blown senile, standing there in the bare 60-watt bathroom lamplight. I was still shaking when I told her I was checking-in, with Lester gone and all. That the family was worried about her. She just said not to worry cause Lester would be back from Canada in a few days. Then she said, "Goodnight, Eddie," and walked me to the door. The wood door was hanging crooked from the top hinge, but old Agnes didn't even notice—just waved goodbye.

I walked back to the Buick, thought about Henry, how everybody said he was buddied up with old Lester Cronin for the last few months of his life. The next morning I didn't even bother to call in sick at the island. I drove downstate to see Johnny at Hillsdale. On the way down, I stopped to see cousin Ryan in Dearborn. His wife Brenda said he was working a double shift at the Ford plant, so I told her I'd swing by there to see him. I emptied the Colt's cylinder and put the rounds in the glove compartment. Never went inside the plant, just drove out to a park on the river outside the plant.

The Colt was wrapped in its blue silk. I stuffed it inside a paper lunch bag and tossed it into the Rouge. Figured it was best that way cause I was itching to use it, Henry's gift to me—the free pass.

I should just walk away from Uncle Pervie. He's so far off, he could never catch me, even if he gimped as fast as he could toward me. I don't have much to lose, though, and he insulted my family. I really do want the book back too. It's pretty damn good and I was thinking about stealing it from the library. Or maybe I just want to kick this guy's ass. Or for him to kick mine—I just don't care either way. He gimp-runs toward me and I walk until we meet by the downtown edge of the bridge.

"Water's cold this time of year," he tells me.

"Don't know about you but I'm not afraid to take a dip," I tell him.

"You related to Gene Metzger?" he asks me.

"What the fuck's it to you?"

Then he starts to size me up. He clinches his fist but he seems to notice that I have the size advantage. I'm taller and outweigh him by fifty pounds, easy. Then I see it—that fear that crazy people get—the same sort of look we used to get in the infantry when we'd drive through some village that was bombed and people would smile, show a lot of teeth, but in their eyes you'd see they want to kill you.

"Think I got the wrong guy. You're not a Metzger, are you? I'm sorry," he tells me.

"I'm your guy," I tell him. "I'm a Metzger. What you want with me."

"No, you're not the guy I'm looking for. I'll just go away."

"Come on now, I thought you were gonna show me how cold it was at the bottom of the canal. Let's swim motherfucker."

Uncle Pervie starts to backpedal toward downtown, watching me with every move. I step toward him and he starts to run. He stops to pick up a rock and he throws it at me. He misses my ear by a couple inches but I feel it snap in the cold air like shrapnel.

"Gonna throw rocks at me you little bitch?" I say. He picks up another and misses again, so far away from me I'm not sure which way it went but I hear the crack and echo behind me on the bridge's walkway. I'm about to turn around and walk away and he hits me with a nickel-sized pebble I didn't see him pick up. Gets me right on my left temple. That's when I run full speed at him.

He takes money out of his wallet with his good hand and throws it in my direction.

"Here, take it," he says. "Leave me alone, man."

He runs while he empties bills from his wallet, his arms jerking side to side.

"Don't want your money. Want to see how you swim," I say.

I would have no problem catching him, but his plan works. First bill I see is a ten and I slow to pick it up. Then, I let him round the corner at Peck Street and I stop altogether to pick up all the bills, thirty-seven dollars total, some of them really crumpled and dirty. His driver's license fell out. It expired twenty years ago and it's scraped up pretty bad but the name's clear, Peter Girard. No wonder he was after me. All the sudden I feel real sober and the wind blows up from the canal and numbs my outer ears. My temple's throbbing and there's blood in my hair and on the side of my face. Time to make the long walk back to my car.

Something's got to change. I need to get off the street. I can sneak a shower at the university tomorrow, try to slip in past security. Got a little extra money now, so might as well drive downtown and park behind the bars on Portage. Got to meet up with Sarah at Maloney's. There's a real stink in the car and I wonder if it's more me or the car. There's an IGA a couple blocks over so I stop there first for some baby wipes. When I was in the Army, we'd have to go weeks at a time without showers when we were in the field or deployed, so we'd bring boxes of baby wipes. Some guys called it a "bitch bath," a few called it a "whore shower." Seemed to do the job, until you got back in garrison, took a real shower, and got a whiff of your clothes. When I'm walking through the in door, I see Blake Braune. I turn my head to the side and try to walk in the opposite direction, like I don't see him, but he sees me.

"Metzger, Buck?"

"Hey, Blake," I say.

"What the fuck happened to you," he says. "You look like shit." He smiles. Blake's glad to see me all fucked up.

"Just got out of work," I say. "Doing construction to save up for college."

"Finished my college last spring," he says. "Trying for the FBI. Meantime, I'm a county deputy."

"Thought I smelled pork," I say.

"Thought I smelled shit when you walked in. Your crew putting in a sewer or is that your new cologne?"

"No, I had a date with your sister after work. Well, wouldn't really call it a date."

Blake tenses up and then he sort of smiles and slaps me on the back. Then he looks at his hand and cringes, wipes it on his pants.

"My sister's in Colorado. Married a banker. Let's catch up—get a couple of drinks."

Last time I saw Mom and Dad, when they kicked me out of the house, Mom was on my case about how I drink too much and the delinquents I'm always hanging around with. She might see Blake as a step up, but he's just as bad as the rest, just hides it better. In fact, he's probably the biggest douchebag I've ever called a friend.

Me and Blake hit Maloney's and he buys us a round of Guinness and single-malt Scotch. Not sure how much it costs, but I buy a round of the same when we finish. The pattern repeats for six rounds and I'm wondering how much this is going to cost, but I got a good enough buzz I don't care too much.

"How'd you ever end up a cop? You're one of the worst lawbreakers I ever met," I say. "How many times you break into the school?"

"I never took anything," he tells me. "Just did it to impress chicks."

"What's your game plan now, arrest 'em, or knock 'em cold with your night stick?"

"Whatever it takes," he says. "Did you hear I'm engaged," he says. "Girl from Florida."

"No. Way to go, you donut-eating fuck," I say. Then he smiles and looks serious.

"It's good to see you, Buck. You're one of the good ones,

even if you smell like shit. Seriously, man. You're one of the best friends I got."

"That's sad," I tell him. "Just fucking with you—you're alright too—for a fucking cop."

"Gotta take a shit," he says. He signals the barmaid for another round. She pretends to ignore him at first, then pours the shots when nobody else is around. The bar's still slow—it's a weeknight and there's no games to watch.

By the time Sarah shows up, I'm pretty trashed. I buy her a drink, put in on my tab, a tab that's too big for me to pay with the cash I have in pocket. She sets *Dubliners* on the bar.

"So, I read some of this at work. It's really good but kind of depressing."

"It's supposed to be."

"What? Depressing or good?"

"Both."

"I have an English minor but I've only had American Literature and Shakespeare so far."

Blake comes back and introduces himself. Makes blowjob gestures behind Sarah's back. I ignore him best I can and stare into Sarah's eyes. They're more soft than I thought they were earlier. She's nervous when we brush together.

"You guys want to grab a coffee with me at Frank's? I got to sober up a little if I'm going to drive back home," Blake says.

"No, I think we'll have a couple more drinks. Maybe catch you later if you're still there," I say.

Blake just smiles and gives me his sign of approval. He pays his tab but doesn't leave a tip. Neither one of us tipped the whole night and the barmaid gives me a bad look when Blake drunk-walks out the door and on to Portage Street. At some point I'm going to have to ask for my tab or ditch. Either way, Sarah can't be around when it happens. She grabs my hand and starts to massage it. Her fingers are softer than they look.

"I'm looking for a relationship with somebody who's deeper, like you, somebody who's complex, passionate."

"You're really great," I tell her. "I don't know if I'm any good for relationships right now though," I tell her. "Need to get my shit together."

Her face sours and she pulls her hand away.

"Fucking asshole," she says. "Should've known. I got to take a piss. Didn't notice before, but you smell like shit, like you slept in a dumpster."

"Thanks," I say. "Dumpster might've been an improvement."

I really got to piss too but I ask the barmaid for the tab.

"Eighty-six bucks," she says, "without tip."

"I've got thirty-six here," I tell her. "The rest is in my car. Let me get it. I swear I'll be right back. Give you a real good tip." I wink at her.

"No, you've got to settle up here or I'm gonna call the manager."

"My name's Pete Girard. I'll be right back with the money."

"Let me see your ID again she says. I remember names and that don't sound right."

"It's right," I tell her and slap Girard's license down at the bar. "Just let me get the money. Promise I'll be right back."

"Don," she yells. "This fucker doesn't want to pay up."

From the corner of my eye, I see Sarah coming back from the bathroom, but she doesn't see me. One quick turn and I'm out the door. Probably won't see Sarah again. For the best though. If she's as good a girl she seems to be, I'll just fuck it up. I'm in no state to fall for somebody. Can't even take care of myself. If I make it back to Maloney's with the money, I might be able to show my face there, so I run left on Portage and turn fast as I can on Osborn past Ridge and Arlington and fall on my ass when I cut through an alley to Spruce Street. I must be more drunk than I thought I was, because I really wiped out and I don't even feel anything. There's blood and ash and mud on my pants. My hands bleed and sting in the cold chill but I wipe myself off and sprint toward the Buick on the other side of town.

There's a tapping on the glass of my car window. I'm so tired I don't want to open my eyes, but I do, just for a second, and I see my brother, Johnny. At first, I think it could really be him, but it must be a dream cause Johnny should be down at Hillsdale. It's a weeknight and it's already basketball season. I hear the tapping again and think it might be a cop or Peter Girard but I look up and see Johnny's face again, so I know it's a dream, but he keeps banging on my car window and my head starts to throb and my eyes burn when I keep 'em open long enough to focus on him. He's wearing his Hillsdale warm-up shirt and a Packers cap. I roll over and the green-covered copy of *Dubliners* bounces off my chest and falls between the brake and gas pedals. My glove box is open with my cash exposed. I turn the key to roll down the driver's side window.

"You drunk son-of-a-bitch," he tells me, "wake up."

"What are you doing up here?" I look at the green letters of my digital clock on the car stereo. It's 4:17 AM.

"They found Grandpa," he says.

"Grandpa Dunleavy? Thought he was still down in Florida."

"Grandpa Metzger," he says. "What's left of him. Come with me. Fucking stinks in here, man. Let's take my car."

I grab my wallet and make sure the envelope with the cash is still in my left front pocket. Don't remember driving, but somehow my car ended-up on Court Street. I lock up the Buick and we hop into Johnny's Delta 88 and head out towards Ashmun.

Few months back, I thought about going to live in Hillsdale with Johnny. He's got a whole dorm room to himself—basketball scholarship pays for it. Everything's going so good for Johnny, though, I didn't want to fuck it up for him. If I lived there rent free, I could've worked a couple jobs and saved for tuition. When Johnny first started there, he talked to the baseball coach about getting me a scholarship. They told me to come down for a try-out but the coach said there's no drinking or smoking during the season. Even give breathalyzers in the dorm when you're least expecting it. It is a Christian school after all. I didn't go. Johnny's the family favorite. I fuck things up for him, none of the family will ever forgive me. One drowning man taking down another, like Uncle Ray always says.

Johnny pulls out toward Ashmun and turns down Portage.

"Some kids were playing in the woods around a provincial park up by Wawa," Johnny says. "They found Grandpa's walking stick poking out the sand, saw the carvings, so they started digging around to see what it was. Nothing but beach, so they kept digging around, scooping out sand with their hands. Then they hit a bone."

"They sure it's him?" I ask.

"The OPP did all kinds of tests on what's left of him, checked his dental records. They're sure it's Grandpa. They even used DNA tests and they say Lester Cronin's the only one could've killed Grandpa, they're ninety-nine percent sure. Found some of Lester's DNA there too. FBI told Grandma that ten years ago they wouldn't have known, but now they're sure with this new technology."

"How can they say for sure?"

"Don't know all the details. Mom told me over the phone. I drove home late and by the time I got there everybody was asleep. Told Dad I'd go look for you. He was still half awake when I came in."

"What'd he say."

"It's about time. Yeah, go get Buck—he needs to know."

"How'd you know where to find me?"

"Followed the smell of rotgut and filthy snatch."

We take Portage drive out to the park by the bait shop under the International Bridge. It's still dark but there's a pink light from the east side of the river.

"Didn't know the West Pier Drive-in was still here," I say.

Johnny pulls a pint bottle of Popov from under his car seat. Holds it out to me.

"Got any water?" I ask him and he hands me a full bottle of Pepsi. It's warm from being so close to the heater but it helps wet my dry mouth. When I get a couple of big drinks out, I nod toward him and tell him, "Put a couple shots in it." We step out into the morning cold and walk down to the river. Last time we were out here was when Johnny's girlfriend dumped him a couple years back and I was home on leave. Didn't say a word, just sat out here and drank beer. Got a couple cheeseburgers from the West Pier and fished until way after dark.

"Remember that time we took the canoe out on the St. Mary's?" Johnny asks.

"Almost got sucked into the wake of that thousand-footer," I say. "Big ass cargo ship."

"We both had to be thinking of that story old Henry and Grandma used to tell us about Jimmy Red Claw."

"How long he hold his breath when he got sucked under that ship out by Barbeau?"

"Close to three minutes, if you believe that story. Then he had to chew his way out of the gill net. Might be a bit of a stretch." We both laugh. I feel less drunk—more alive. But I'm still tired.

"We got to do something about this Cronin situation. Can't do it without you, brother. Come home."

For the last four years, there's nothing I've wanted more than to come home. To make something of myself. To set things right. To get revenge for what Cronin did to Grandpa Eddie. Thought about it so much in the Army, almost got myself killed a couple times. One time, almost got run over by one of our own Bradleys when I was holding security in the prone. So much damned noise, didn't even hear the thing and he sure as shit didn't see me. This guy from the platoon, Levy, grabbed my BDU collar and peeled my body from the ground, just in time to avoid the tracks. Would've at least ripped my legs off, but I'm sure he saved my life. He was smaller than Johnny, kind of a midget, but there was something about his confidence that always reminded me of Johnny.

For the first time I can remember, Johnny doesn't look so confident.

"Let's talk," I say. "We'll come up with a plan—plenty of time. Hey, you'll never guess who I saw last night. Pete Girard."

"Who's Pete Girard?"

"A man who's lucky to be alive, even if he's missing a few parts. I'll let the old man tell you about him. Swing by Maloney's with me—got a debt to pay. Then we'll walk down to Frank's for breakfast—should be open."

Johnny stops pacing and squats down next to me, slaps me on the back. Then he goes back to pacing.

"Give me just a minute," he says. His breath fogs over the St. Mary's River, fades into the cold sunrise and damp air.

A tugboat sets out for Lake Superior from the Canadian side of the locks. The current slaps the oak breakwall under Johnny's feet and smog rolls in from the paper mill to change the taste of our air. Johnny looks like he's in a trance until seagulls start to squawk and circle over the river. He takes a deep breath and nods to the Oldsmobile.

1984

The kitchen window facing the elms and north stretch of highway is fogged and dark like puffs of smoke from Grandma's brown cigarette. Steam water hisses under the lid of the three-gallon stew pot and the red teapot whistles from the back left burner. Comet and mop water drown out the smell of roast chuck and potatoes. Grandma tops off her coffee with Kessler's and hides the bottle behind ten-pound bags of flour and sugar.

"I killed your grandpa," she says. Doesn't smile or get teary-eyed, just keeps a straight face.

"You weren't even there," I say.

"Should've let him rot in jail. Bailed him out too soon. If he would've been locked up another two weeks, he never would've gone to Canada with Lester Cronin."

There's a chill from the chipped linoleum floor that runs up my legs. They must be letting the fire burn out to clean the ashes. The only heat in the room comes from the kitchen oven. Grandma puts another black pot on the stove with kielbasa, then cracks half a dozen eggs in the frying pan on the left front burner. She always makes her eggs over easy and she's the only one who can do it perfect without the yolk running all over.

"I love him. We had our problems and everybody thinks I'm happier without him, but I'm not."

"Nobody thinks that," I tell her.

"Get out to the barn. Help your Uncle Ray," she says. "I'll bring breakfast out to the porch when the eggs are done." She lights another cigarette and stares out the new picture window, south, toward the garage.

The rust-gold thermometer rail-spiked to the inside barn wall says forty degrees, a warm day for January. Icicles hang from the tin roof over the main door and drip into slush puddles on the concrete entry way. The tall, gray packing crate full of cedar butts is on top of another tall crate, so I need the ladder. Dad told me to split half a cord for Grandma, but I'm not sure how many pieces make up a cord. Some of the butts are thick and heavy, so I have a hard time getting my gloves around 'em. Other pieces are only big around as a baseball bat. I try to throw as many down, fast as I can, but the whole thing is a backwards puzzle—you have to take out one piece before you get the next. They're packed in the crate good, and some are still iced together. I throw down what looks like a few wheelbarrow loads and climb down for the axe.

Grandma and Uncle Ray are just outside the barn door. They're trying to figure out what to do with Silas, Grandpa's old stock horse. He started limping around the last couple of weeks. Might be from the accident or it could be age—he's older than I am, and that's old in horse years.

"Take him out past the wheat field," Grandma says. She hands Ray the old black .38 pistol with a wooden handle.

"He'll make it okay," says Ray. "Just got a little limp. It gets worse, I'll put him out in a couple weeks."

"Dammit Ray," she says, "I'll do it myself. We both know he ain't gonna make it through winter. Might as well do it now."

Grandma's purple sweatshirt is mostly clean, with just a few drops of snow drizzle on her shoulders. Her black pants are neat and pressed except for the wet muddy cuffs that cover her brown slip-on shoes. She's got full-size pink rollers pinned in her black hair and she wants to get back to the house to take care of inside business. She stares down Ray till he looks toward the crates of cedar butts.

"Too much work today, Ma. By the time I clean up the mess, dig a hole and bury Silas proper-"

Ray's brown flannel jacket and black jeans are covered in two weeks of grime. He's got a green helmet liner for a hat and tan leather mitts instead of gloves. Grandma puffs smoke into Ray's face from her cigarette to tell him she's serious.

"You got Buck here to help you out. You dig the hole and I'll get a tarp for the mess." They turn back toward the garage.

"Don't do it Ray." I yell out the door. "It's just a limp."

"Mind your business, Buck," says Grandma.

"Give me the pistol," says Ray. "If it's gotta be done, I'm gonna do it. Get in there and chop some kindlin', Buck."

Out the barn door you can almost see the sunrise under the cotton gray. Every few minutes, a gust from the north blows in sideways through the wide open wall. Some of the butts split easy. Hit 'em clean a couple times and they fall in fire-sized splinters on the cement floor. Other pieces split crooked and you have to pull everything apart once the axe gets stuck. Sometimes you got no choice but beat the wood on the cement just to get the axe free.

If I had another ten dollars, I'd be skiing with Katherine Beckett. She was begging me to go all week, staring soft at me with those deep blue eyes. Never been downhill skiing before. Probably never will the ways things are around here. If I had the money, Mom and Dad would have another excuse—don't want me to break an arm before baseball season—or there's too much work around the house. Or Grandma's house. It's the second time I had to lie to Katherine—the truth is too embarrassing. We were supposed to talk about a book on the bus to Boyne Mountain. *A Farewell to Arms.* Katherine loves two things: sports and books. She's so good at tennis she even beats most the high school girls. But books she loves even more than tennis—always reading something. Katherine smells like lilacs and her hair is never out of place. She's kind of a pain in the ass when she gets bossy, but it feels good to be around her.

The .38 shot echoes out over the wheat field.

Maybe it's better I didn't go skiing. I only got 199 pages into the book. Katherine says it's a love story but it seems more like a war story to me. The part where I left off talks about a muddy old farm road with water overflowing on the sides, kind of like the dirt and limestone road out to the pond by the wheat field. I'll finish the book by Monday, but my job for now is cedar butts.

I almost got a wheelbarrow full when I hear the side door to the stable open and the metal bolt clang against the wall. Uncle Ray climbs up to the loft and comes down with a tire iron. He's about to go back through the side door but he turns and looks at me.

"What the hell you think you're doing?" He says, "If you

do it right, you don't have to beat the piss out the floor with cedar butts. Give me the axe."

The tire iron clangs on the concrete by the stable door. The ponies and horses stomp and whinny.

Ray splits a few butts and they come apart clean and straight.

"This is how it's done, see? You fill up the wheelbarrow and take the kindlin' to the woodshed. Bring some inside for the old lady. I'll split—you're taking too damn long. Gonna break the fuckin' concrete."

The axe gets stuck halfway down on his next chop. I laugh kind of quiet when Ray pries it loose from the cedar butt and the handle slips and hits his leg. He sees me but I don't care—it's hard to respect a man who puts down an innocent horse. Especially a guy who spends so much time in church and always preaches to everybody else what's right and moral. Ray is solid most the time, but sometimes he scares the hell out of me. He's only half the weight of Uncle Jack but he's got the strength of most guys three times his size and a blastfurnace temper. Even though the yellow wheelbarrow's only three quarters full, I move as fast as I can to the house. I'm almost there when Ray curses something at me but I keep walking with my back towards him. I push the load up to the porch, grab an armload of kindling and turn the brass knob.

I peek in the kitchen from the entryway but Grandma's not there. I walk an armful of kindling through the kitchen and the hall to the living room, and pile the cedar sticks by the fireplace. There's a black water trail from my boots on the cracked-white kitchen floor. I go for her mop in the back part of the house. It's already in my hands when she yells, "I just cleaned the damned floor. Get the mop."

Father Pierre stopped by earlier but Grandma went upstairs and left me and Uncle Ray to handle him. The priest told us it's time to consider a memorial for Grandpa. Ray told him Grandpa's coming back, that he's lost in the woods in Canada and he'll find his way cause he's a survivor. Ray told Father Pierre his services weren't needed unless he wanted to give Silas a proper sendoff. Father said that animals don't have souls, so there's no point. Then he just rolled his eyes and drove off in his rusted blue Fairlane. Grandpa always said you could never trust clergy in a convertible. Most the family was up by Wawa for over a week to look for Grandpa after he went missing. Dad, Tony and Ray stayed on another week but didn't find anything. The OPP said they'd call when they heard something. Dad says the only one gonna save Grandpa if he's alive is Grandpa.

It's Saturday. Since I'm not skiing I could be at the field downtown playing snow football with the guys. Since Grandpa disappeared, Dad sends me over to help Grandma with chores a couple times a week. Woke me up today at 6:30 when everybody else was still sleeping and dropped me off here. Asked him why Johnny wasn't coming but Dad says my brother's too young to help. I don't buy it. He's ten already. I asked Dad why I couldn't sleep in and help out later in the day and he just said, "Move your ass, we're burning daylight."

When I got to Grandma's this morning, she was already awake for a while. She was smoking, reading some old Russian novel. Now she's in the living room with a push vacuum, scraping up the dirt on the old brown carpet, still got the pink curlers in her hair.

"Fire's out. Start another one and put the rest of the kindling there. Gonna get cold later."

"Where's Ray gonna bury Silas?" I ask her.

"Out past the duck pond," she says. "Told him to throw some stone on top so the coyotes don't dig him up."

"He would've made it through the winter," I tell her.

"Other night I had a dream about my papa," Grandma says. "When we were kids, we used to spend the summer at that log cabin out on the Fox River. No lights. No water. Blocks of ice in sawdust to keep the food fresh."

"No water? You were next to a river."

"No plumbing's what I mean, wiseass. You're already a trouble-maker and you ain't even hit puberty yet. Why can't you be more like little Johnny. Should get yourself a decent haircut like your brother. Now that's a sweet kid."

"My brother Johnny?"

"That's right."

"You don't know him."

"But I know you. On track to end up like your old man, you are. Anyways—sometimes I get to thinking about things that happened when I was a little girl and I panic. I want to know the name of some neighbor from down the street—I see the face clear but not the name—and I think to ask my papa, but then it hits me I can't. He's gone. Just like Ma. Almost everyone from back then. It's like the claustrophobia but with time, and there's no way to get back. You're too young to understand. Once you been in this world for some time, you stop and look around and twenty years gone by like nothing. As much as you want to, there's no going back."

She lights a brown cigarette and inhales deep. Then she takes a drink from a glass bottle of Squirt. I saw her pour Kessler's into that same bottle this morning when she thought nobody was looking.

"Used to think people had all the answers by the time they're my age. Sometimes I'm less sure now than when I was a kid. Almost everybody older than me is gone now. Don't take family for granted, that's all I got to say."

"You think they'll ever find Grandpa?" I ask her.

"Get yourself some apple crisp and clear your plate when you're done. Then I need you to carry some boxes upstairs for me."

Kindling's stacked waist high in the barn. Ray chopped enough cedar to fill the shed and then some. My jean cuffs are soaked from slushing back and forth with the wheelbarrow. The sun is out and the ice water from the roof of the barn drips faster. The thermometer says it's fifty degrees now. The orange, county truck plows ice slush from the meridian highway on the west side of Grandma's house. Ray walks toward the barn with a pickaxe.

"Smell that?" he says. "Fuckin' skunk. Get a shovel and go clean it up."

"You sure? I don't smell anything," I tell him.

"Coming from over there, by the apple trees. Take a corn bag and bury it out by the field."

"Why don't you do it?"

"Don't backtalk me, do as you're told. I gotta bury Silas out by the pond, less you wanna change jobs. Get the skunk and by the time we finish, we'll meet up here and clean the barn mess."

When Ray turns toward the gravel road and heads off to dig a hole for Silas, I pull the screen door open and step back into the breezeway of Grandma's house. Grandma's pulling a gallon bucket of turkey gravy from out of the deep freeze. She runs hot water over the lid while she pries the bottom of the circle with a paring knife. The steam from the sink re-fogs the back kitchen window.

Wind from the north rattles the screen against the window glass. "So much for the heat wave," she says, her back to me. "We'll see more snow by dinner. There's another box in the living room needs up to the attic."

"Anything else you want while I'm in here?"

"Take the brown box upstairs to the back room. Get yourself a Hershey's bar and a cup of cocoa on your way back out."

There's a photo album on top of the box. First picture inside is clear black and white with pink stains around the edges. Three men by an old car. Looks like a Model-T, like the old folks drive around on the Fourth of July. Fat guy on the left wears a suit and a derby. The skinny guy in middle and the guy with a curly moustache on the right are both smoking pipes.

"One in the middle's your Great-Grandpa, Nate."

"What year is this," I ask her.

"Twenties. Maybe nineteen twenty-two, three. Don't know the man on the right. Think it's a relative. Man on the left is Al Acciaio. My papa worked with him. Used to come over for dinner when I was a little girl. Gave me this." She pulls a gold locket and chain out the box.

"What kind of work," I ask.

"Papa was in transportation. Had his own company. When I was a little girl, we ate off real silver. Lived in the biggest house on the block. White columns, red brick."

"What was that like?"

"That was a long time back. Never did laundry or washed dishes till I got married. My papa died in forty-eight and everything changed."

"How'd he die?"

"Get that box upstairs and go help Ray."

Every few minutes, a gust blows through and reminds me it's January. My eyes water from the skunk. I brushed up against the tail, so now my jeans are skunked. Grandma won't want me in the house smelling like this. Missed my snack break cause that son-of-a-bitch Ray drug me out of the kitchen. Told Grandma, "No breaks for Buck till he gets rid of the skunk."

Even with two bags around the carcass, the smell's gonna be too much. I toss the bags and shovel into the wheelbarrow and walk it toward the wet asphalt. Wonder if Ray finished with Silas yet. That was the best horse I ever knew. I'd like to shovel Ray upside the head for putting a bullet in him, especially since Father Pierre said Silas don't have a soul. Ray didn't even give that horse a chance.

Silas saved Grandpa once, when he was pinned down by that elm tree back at his hunting cabin. It was rotten from the elm disease and didn't fall the way he thought it would. Silas trotted right over to him, like he knew. Gramps grabbed the left stirrup and Silas worked him loose. Then Gramps pulled himself up into the saddle and that old horse took him twelve miles home. Reason Silas got a limp is Ray run him into an old barb-wire fence a few weeks ago. I saw when it happened. Ray really got some nerve to put a bullet between that horse's ears.

Least Silas didn't suffer like this skunk. Looks like the skunk made it about fifty feet without its hind legs before it curled up and died by the driveway. There's a blood trail through the slush on the Meridian all the way to here. What's left of the back legs is flat on the road. Stinks all the way up to the Chippewa County line. You couldn't pay me all the silver and gold coins Grandma has to clean this up, but I have to do it for free. There was a whole box of old things she had me bring down from upstairs. Said some of the coins were from when she was a little girl, but most of it they found when they moved into the house in the fifties. The house was here since the 1800's, so it was already old when they moved back from downstate. Grandma says they were fixing up the foundation and they had to take out old rotten beams from the cellar. When Grandpa and his brothers were crawling around down there, they found a metal box in the dirt under a beam. It had all the coins and some old yellow papers. Grandma says you never know what you'll find when you get to digging around.

Hope I'll get that lucky one of these days. Don't want to spend the rest of my life cleaning up skunks and chopping kindling.

"Quit daydreaming and clean up the damned skunk," Uncle Ray says. "Almost lunch time. Let's finish up."

He opens up the burlap corn bag and nods to my shovel. I tuck most of my face under my green sweatshirt and scrape the skunk from gravel and slush. I lift the carcass to the bag but a few chunks of red and yellow skunk innards fall off the shovel. The skunk head rolls out but Ray kicks it into the bag with his rawhide work boot.

"Get all of it," he says. "Those pieces there too. Don't leave none of it on the driveway."

"Can't get all of it," I tell him. "He's stuck to the ground."

"Get as much as you can," says Ray. "Don't give me that look. You got someplace better to be?"

"I could be skiing," I tell him.

Ray starts laughing like I never seen him laugh before. "Skiing. Well excuse me."

"Was gonna go with the school. You get a discount. Just needed ten more dollars."

"Where they go skiing?"

"Boyne Mountain. It's downstate, across the bridge."

"I know where it is," he says. "Deliver lumber down there sometimes. Don't even get me started on that. Why the hell you wanna go there?"

"Some of my friends go and they say it's cool. What's wrong with Boyne?"

"Not Boyne, that whole fuckin' place. Don't care to see anything south of the Mackinac Bridge."

"Why? You were born in Detroit."

"Not my fault. I was just a baby back then. You get down there, they don't even put the U.P. on the map. Nothing but the fuckin' mitt. They can keep all that—everything under the bridge. Fine with me if I never cross the Straits the rest of my life."

We walk through the limestone sludge down the old road to the woods on the far side of the field. The wind is picking up and the sun is under the clouds now. When we get to the treeline, it calms a bit, with the hardwoods blocking the cold breeze. I helped Grandpa take back a blue spruce from here, Christmas before last. Around the pond there's all kinds of evergreens, but Gramps always liked spruce best. That Christmas tree smell always comes out, even over skunk.

"Where did you bury Silas?"

"Other side of the pond," he says. "Not finished yet. Need a big hole. Man, Silas was a monster."

"Why'd you shoot him? He would've made the winter."

"I didn't," he says. "Your Grandma did."

I start to dig a hole for the skunk behind the barn but the dirt's still frozen hard. When I get a foot down, Ray says, "Good job. Tough ground." He takes the shovel and starts to work the earth. "Wash off the skunk and help your Grandma. She's in the garage. I'll finish this up."

Katherine and the kids from school are still down at Boyne. Won't get home till long after I shower and the coyotes start to circle Silas. Katherine says skiing's a real workout but I bet it's nothing like all the running around, lifting, chopping and wheelbarrow pushing I've been doing today. Even the boxes of albums and pictures Grandma had me hauling up and down are starting to kick my ass.

I remember where I heard the name Al Acciaio before. Last summer, when Tony Vega, Grandpa, Dad and Duke Moreau were playing a game of Spitzer, Tony said Acciaio was a "murderin' bootlegger," just like his old man. Acciaio's grandson has a hunting cabin down Webb Road and Tony and Dad played cards with him a couple deer seasons ago. Wonder why Great Grandpa Nate would know this Acciaio? Tony had a mouthful of chopped beef and crackers and started telling us about his own grandpa—how they made a tunnel under the border from Texas to Mexico to run liquor. He said the whiskey and tequila paid for the Vega family ranch.

I wonder if Katherine's family has these kinds of friends. Can't imagine they'd like all these killers, crooks and bootleggers, the kind of people that my family always takes in.

Grandma moved on to butchering duties in the garage and I'm helping out. She couldn't find where Ray left the axe, so she told me to fetch the cleaver. Says Uncle Jack wants to butcher all the livestock and give away the ponies and horses. Jack told her if Grandpa ain't coming back, he's not taking care of 'em anymore. A pony stepped on Jack's foot last week and broke three of his toes. That's when he told Grandma there was no good reason to keep the animals and that his farming days were done. Ranch life was Grandpa's dream. Almost nobody else in this town does it. Jack says everybody knows the soil's no good for growing either. It's too cold and the land's too hard.

Jack's alright, but he's got a temper almost as bad as Uncle Ray. When he gets riled up, he always wants to wrestle or slap me around. He's got about a hundred pounds on me so it's never a fair fight. There's a lot of hate inside him, not like Ray. He's okay to have around though—nobody at school messes with me cause of Jack. Some high school kids were picking on me and Johnny after school last March. We were waiting for basketball practice and got hungry, so we walked down to the Bon Air to get cheese and crackers. We just turned the corner to Hodeck Street and Scotty Kilgore was standing behind the bait shop, by the dock, smoking weed in his corncob pipe with Timmy Muller and some short guy with glasses. Scotty started asking for our money. He got close enough I could smell the rotgut on his fat red face. His eyes were bloodshot and his long, stringy-orange hair was in a sloppy ponytail. He grabbed me by the collar when Jack pulled up in Ray's pickup. All Jack said was, "Fucked up real bad this time, Kilgore." The short fat guy said, "What you gonna do about it?" Jack smacked the glasses off the guy's face with his backhand and made his nose bleed. Then he grabbed Scotty's fat throat under his wiry-red beard and choked him one-handed. Timmy Muller wanted to start some shit but Jack held up his left fist and Timmy stepped back. "These boys are my nephews," Jack said. "You don't touch my kin, get that." Then he jabbed Scotty on his chin with his left fist. Scotty choked out a yes. Jack jabbed him twice more on the chin even though Scotty said, "Yes." Then he asked him if he got it six more times, each time followed-up with a left-hand slap. When he let go of Scotty's throat, Timmy gave me and Johnny a bad look. "I don't think you get it," Jack told him. "If anybody touches these guys again, you'll put an end to it, or I'll end you." Then Scotty's eyes watered up. "We're done here," Jack said. He watched me and Johnny walk back to the gym, quiet and hungry. Me and Johnny always wondered if he did it for us or he just wanted a reason to beat the piss out of Scotty.

Jack used to go at it with Grandpa, not physical—mostly yelled at each other. Dad says Jack got away with it cause he was the baby. Grandpa never would've let it go with the older boys. Since Gramps is gone, Jack started in, always teasing and fighting with

Grandma. He really tries to bully her but she doesn't usually pay him attention cause she's drinking as much whiskey as Grandpa did. When I walk back in the garage with the cleaver, Grandma's slamming a triple shot right from the bottle. Looks like she's ready for another till she hears me and hides the half gallon jug in a wooden milk crate.

"Can I get a shot of that?" Didn't see Lester Cronin's truck pull in on my way back to the garage. It's like he popped out of nowhere and now he's standing in the front corner of the garage, by the bench where Grandpa keeps his engine parts.

"What you need, Lester?" Grandma asks him with her back turned. "We're busy round here."

"Thought I might be of service, Eddie still missing and all."

"We're managing just fine," she says, "and he'll be back before long."

"Them Canadian woods is a tough place. He don't make it back, want you to know I'm always around."

"We don't need you round here, Lester," Grandma tells him. "Agnes expecting you?" Grandma takes a chop at the last turkey's neck with her cleaver. It's not a clean cut and the turkey makes a noise I never heard a turkey make, while he kicks his legs and flaps his feathers. Grandma keeps his head steady on the upside-down steel bucket. She finally hacks the neck clean off after another three dirty cleaver chops.

"Never seen a purty lady do that," says Lester.

"Daddy taught me."

Uncle Jack comes in from the side door with a flathead screwdriver in his left coat pocket and a carburetor cradled in his right arm. He looks at Grandma and gives Lester the same look he gave Scotty Kilgore.

"You best head out, Cronin," he says.

"I'm awful sorry 'bout your old man." Lester smirks and winks at Grandma. "Just making sure the old lady's okay. Your old man would want it that way."

Jack's forehead gets redder and the veins in his temple stand out blue like wiper fluid leaking down the sides of a plastic jug. He opens the door and points Lester out.

"We got family business to attend," Grandma says. "I'll send Ray if we need your help."

Then she looks at me.

"There's a five dollar bill for you on the kitchen counter." She takes the Kessler's from the milk crate and swigs from the bottle with her left hand while she puffs her cigarette with the right. "Let's go back to the house."

Lester smirks at the three of us and lingers around for a few seconds before he walks out to his pickup. He cranks his diesel engine and drives off before Jack can close the shop door.

"You don't need to give me money," I tell Grandma on the way to the house.

"It's from your Uncle Ray."

"Dad says you don't take money for favors. Not for helping family."

"Just take the damn thing," she says. "You take care of family, family takes care of you. Ray says to save up for the next ski trip. Try not to stink up my kitchen. Tell you what, I'll get the money for you and a couple cans of tomato juice. You get home and take a bath—still smell like skunk piss."

In Grandma's box of albums, I saw another picture of Great Grandpa Nate with Great Grandma Marie and Grandma when she was a kid. Grandma was about five or six-years-old. Her family was all sitting on the steps of a house with long white pillars. She looks so different now, except her eyes. The shine in her eyes never changed over the years. Even in that kid picture she looks wise as a Grandma.

"Second thought, before you head home, why don't you go check on Ray. Might need Jack too. That's a big horse."

At least Grandma's telling her stories, making jokes again. Didn't say more than three words to me when I came to help last week. Winter's long from over, though, and she might get worse before things get better. The wind's picking up stronger when I step out the front door of the house and the temperature's dropping fast. It's early but the sun's almost down. Jack must still be working in the garage. There's a light on in the back, but I take a shovel from the front of the garage without calling for him and head back into the cold. Don't want to get too comfortable with the heat from the gas stove.

When Ray told me Grandma killed Silas, I felt kind of sorry for Ray. She really put him in a bad spot. I'm ready to help Ray finish the hole, but by the time I get there, he's got a full canyon dug. Everybody in the family works hard but none of them can outshovel Ray.

"Just coming to get you," says Uncle Ray. "Look what I found down there." He pulls a gray-black-haired skull out from a canvas bag and holds it arm's length from my face, screaming before he laughs.

"Is that real?" I ask him. My chest cools and I get a tingling down my back.

"He's been here a while. Don't even stink no more. Green coat ripped apart when I pulled out the arm bone. Couldn't figure out what the hell it was when the pick hit it. Knew it wasn't a rock."

"Where's the rest of him."

"Most of him's in the bag. He's scattered around. Get your shovel—maybe they buried something good with him."

"You sure this is a good idea? Seems like bad luck."

"They didn't bury him Christian anyhow. Asides, I'm down here pretty damn deep and I ain't digging another hole for Silas today. Everybody knows it's not right to bury your horse with a strange man."

"Okay, but I'm not touching the bones," I tell him.

Ray's face is red-cold and he's got a frostbite grin while he digs around for the rest of the skeleton. He stops digging when we both see the dull shine from the near side of Ray's horse trench.

"DNR badge." Ray wipes dirt from another patch of what's left of the skeleton's coat and collared shirt. He gets pale and serious and after about a minute goes by with his mouth open, he says, "Wade Hamilton."

"Can't be," I say. "Thought he got transferred to Negaunee."

"Twenty-six years back," Ray says. "That was the story."

Ray stares out toward the gray clouds and the pink-sky sunset for a while, then he gets back to digging out smaller parts and cloth pieces.

"Damn, you smell like skunk," Ray says, pulling up a foot bone. "Looks like the last of this skeleton."

The wind slows and snow starts to fall in sloppy wet flakes. "Good enough. Run and get Jack. Let's put Silas in this hole. That storm's a coming."

"What about that," I point to the brown canvas bag.

"Got a delivery to make in Naubinway tomorrow. I'll drop old Wade off over the Cut River bridge. We'll keep this between you, me and Jack, got it? Your Grandma's got enough to worry about—doesn't need these old bones to set her back."

1994

Our post is in the hilly, wooded area outside the city. We sleep and eat in an old stone building with dirt floors. There's no electricity or running water, so we shower at a bigger camp, the command center outside a small town just south of Sarejevo. Stubb, Perry and Morgan were just there last week, so they don't stink as much as the rest of us. For Robinson, Wiggins, Van Dorn and me, it was three weeks since our last shower and it might be another two or three weeks before the next one. Our BDUs are woodland camouflage but they turn white after a while with all the sweat salt. Even though it's still kind of rocky where we are, it's green and the trees don't look too different from the ones back home. A small river curves around the greener side of the hill. Sometimes we dip our feet in it to clean 'em up. Robinson and Wiggins won't do it cause the water's too cold, but it doesn't bother me any—it's warmer than Lake Superior in the spring. We did get some supplies—ammo, MREs, and water but no soap this time.

In our deployment briefing, Major Hansen said Sarajevo used to be one of the most beautiful cities in eastern Europe. Said it's the place where World War I started and the people here sided with the Nazis in World War II. Got lucky here though—they didn't bomb the hell out of it like some parts of Europe. We've been here two months and most of what we see is country roads and hills. Gets confusing sometimes, who's fighting who, with Serbs and Croats and everyone else. We're not a real unit, just a small attachment manning a lookout station for the UN to make sure they don't all kill each other. Our whole company is scattered around the hills and valleys, mixed in with others units. We just report any fighting we see. It's not our war.

Some guys think Bosnia looks like the places we trained in Colorado and New Mexico, except maybe greener. To me, it reminds me of the places Hemingway talks about in his books, like WWI Italy or the mountains in Spain. Except for yesterday, it's been mostly quiet, kind of boring. This morning we had the first hot meal in a week, thanks to the Sterno we brought back last night. Everything else lately's been MREs and every box we get is missing the number five meal—spaghetti. The command center guys always steal the good meals before they make it to the field, the ones with M&Ms. Most of our hot meals come from cans, the kind of rations Dad probably ate in Vietnam.

When we got to Europe, they started breaking up the units based on needs. Wiggins and Robinson are from a transportation unit. Van Dorn is logistics. We didn't know any of them before coming here, but Stubb, Perry and Morgan are from my infantry company. You get to know people real fast though, when you're deployed. We're not technically on a combat mission, we're more of a security force, but they wanted a lot of combat arms guys here because they think this whole mess might explode soon and then we'll be ready. In the meantime, we just mostly watch. There really isn't a whole lot of action and we're not supposed to fire our weapons unless we get clearance from higher up.

Wiggins talks the most about killing. It's kind of funny since he's a transportation guy. Most of us infantry guys don't even mention it, except for Perry. We just stay quiet, observe and report. Do our job. One day, Wiggins was going on and on about how much "Euro-trash he was gonna smoke" until Robinson threatened to choke him if he didn't shut up. Then Wiggins started getting on Robinson's case, calling him an Oreo pussy, until Captain Stubb ordered both of them to clean the perimeter for the rest of the day. After an hour, Wiggins started running his mouth again and Stubb gave him all the shit duties—latrine, trash, double night duty for two weeks. He told Robinson to take a break and cool off. Then he told Wiggins to stop acting like a wigger. Then he said, "Wiggins—wigger!" and laughed for a good couple of minutes like he never thought of it before.

Wiggins just said, "That's racist, Sir! That's some fucked up shit. Why you wanna do me like that?"

Wiggins told me later that Stubb better never show his face in Oakland, cause when he's out of the Army, he'll be gunning for him. Told me why he signed up. He was in a gang back in Oakland and arrested for assault. Said it wasn't his fault—when you live in some neighborhoods, you just grow up part of the gang. He got caught and the judge gave him the option of military or jail time. Not sure how much to believe—the guy's full of bullshit most the time, but he looked me in the eyes when he told me all of this and he seemed real serious. The part I know for sure is that he would've killed Captain Stubb without blinking if he could've got away with it. Says the only people like Stubb in Oakland are in the bottom of dumpsters.

Back in garrison, a lot of people like Wiggins are always talking about wanting action and getting deployed. Funny how the people with the biggest mouths are always the first ones crying or pissing their pants when it actually happens. Since the first Gulf War, the rest of the world thinks everything's gotten peaceful but there's always some kind of shit going down. Seems like we're always on alert, locked down in the barracks. Most of the time, nothing happens and we just keep on our business. Then one day you're on a plane to some shithole mess. I remember my first deployment. Everybody thought it was a drill and they didn't even pack all their gear cause there were so many close calls in the months leading up to it. Lot of grunts ended up leaving important personal shit behind.

Then you're deployed and all anybody talks about is back home. Most days here are slow, just like back in garrison. We play a lot more cards here and just talk—about women, music and whatever else comes up. Sometimes you almost lose yourself in the cards and the bullshit—forget you're a soldier deployed in some foreign country, until somebody starts shooting at you or launching grenades, or you run into people who talk funny and dress funny and you realize you can't understand a damn word they're saying.

We told Stubb, Perry and Morgan a few stories about the ambush yesterday. In Wiggins' version of the story, he didn't piss his pants. Now we're back to playing Spades under flashlight. Wiggins, Robinson and me all brought cloth folding stools with us to Bosnia. We're used to spending time in the field. Van Dorn's mostly a clerk and wasn't expecting to be here, so he's stuck sitting on a five-gallon water can. He shifts every few minutes when the handle makes skin dents in his ass cheeks. Our table is a four-high stack of MRE boxes.

"Got a buddy attached to third platoon Bravo," Wiggins says. "'Bout once a month, he come back up in the barracks after he be hanging out with the girls on the south side, syphilis all over his face and shit. All brave when it come to pussy but he a bitch when it comes to firefights—those mortars, getting shot at and all that. Mofucker would've shit his tighty-whities last night."

"There's a dude like that in my platoon. Sisco. Except he's smart enough to wrap his shit up," I say. "This dude's got so much porn on VHS, so many stacks of titty mags, his quarters looks like the back room of a truck stop. Can't shoot for shit. 11B and he needs a shooter in the knoll just to make Marksman."

"We got another dude, Ramirez," Robinson says, "got all that and blow-up dolls, handcuffs, all kinds of kinky shit up in the barracks. Room look like a damn medieval dungeon."

We're laughing so hard we hardly notice Van Dorn shaking. He left his cards face up on the MRE table. He's over by the edge of the hill.

"We almost died last night," Van Dorn says.

"But we didn't," Wiggins says. He clears his sinuses and spits out toward the downslope side of the hill.

Van Dorn dry heaves till he pukes.

Since we're a combat arms mission and we don't have much contact with regular civilians, I haven't seen a woman in over three months. It's bad enough back at the barracks with guys talking about jerking off all the time, but it's worse here, living like wild animals. Most the guys here just whip it out in front of you and start jerking it like it's no big deal, the way most guys piss in the woods. I still can't bring myself to do that. Perry's doing it out in the open right now. Looks like he's having a seizure—it all reminds me that we're still in Bosnia and I want to get the fuck out of here.

My hands are shaking again. I really need a drink. Didn't notice the shaking before—all the laughing helps you forget for a while.

Van Dorn said last night's the first time he's been shot at. Probably not the case for Robinson and definitely not for Wiggins. Today wasn't the first time I've been shot at either. Hell, I got shot at before I enlisted, down in Detroit, when my cousin Ryan and me ended-up in the wrong neighborhood. Couple of close calls at the Iraq border a few years back, when I first came in. Some of the guys, big, tough-talking guys, were crying for their mommas at night. This one time, we were in a safe area. Nobody ever came by to give us ammo. We were set up around a re-supply camp, like the UN base fifty kilometers from here. One night a couple Crimson Guards caught this big guy, Samuels, sleeping, standing up, on guard duty. They would've fired on him with their AKs, but one of 'em pulled a knife, so they could kill him quiet. The second Samuels felt the knife coming in he knocked the Iraqi out cold and grabbed his M-16 on instinct. The other dude panicked when his AK misfired, so he dropped it and put his hands in the air to surrender. Backed away and then tried to run when he saw the look in Samuels' eyes. Samuels caught up to him and butted him in the back with the stock of his sixteen. Ended-up strangling both of them to death. Killed them with his bare hands, like he would always say.

"After last night, I wanna go get some action, don't know 'bout y'all," Wiggins says.

"If it's up to me, I hope we don't hear one more shot the whole time we're here," I say.

"Spoken like a true pussy," Wiggins says.

"Keep running your mouth and you'll be back on the latrines," I tell him.

"Damn, why you got to pull rank on me Metzger? Thought we was cool—why you gotta go there?"

"I hope you get your action, Wig," I tell him. "Just hope I'm long gone from here when those bullets start to fly around your head. Don't want to be the one stuck cleaning up the mess."

My step-grandpa, Colonel Henry saw more than his share of action and he always said a man who couldn't hold his own in a fight was worth nothing but a man who goes looking for a fight is a damn fool. Wiggins is a bullshitter but he's no fool.

1984

Hot red lines from Blake's nostrils steam in the frozen air and roll down into his mouth. My wrist throbs but I swing again, my gloved hand in a sloppy half-fist, thumping his purple left cheek. Blake takes a shot at my head but I move enough that he only gets the bottom of my face. Ronnie LeVasseur grabs my arm before I can swing back. My chin burns and pulses in the cold, and the gust from the north stings my bare ears. Blake laughs. I show him the killer eye and tell him to come get some more. The bump on his nose turns black and he spits blood in the snow bank. Blake tries to swing at me again, but Jay Creekmore grabs the back of his coat and makes him trip on the ice. Everyone in the circle around us laughs at him, even Chelsea, his girlfriend.

"Hope it was worth it, Buck fuck," he says. "Turning on your friends for a fucking retard."

I look over to Malcolm. His thick brown frames are snapped where the black electrical tape used to hold them together. He grips the two pieces of broken frame in his hands, still kicking and crying on the icy sidewalk like a baby.

"Get up," I tell him. "Be a man, Malcolm."

The blood on his face is dark red, like the bricks of the school behind him. It's clotted, frozen raw on his ears and lips—everywhere—except for the bright gush from his nose and the pink stains on his cheeks where the tears are running down. He smiles and says, "Okay, Buck."

He tries to get up from the sidewalk but his blue-flannelled sleeve is stuck to the ice and his feet skid out from under him. Most of the kids laugh. Malcolm smiles but doesn't know why.

Mr. Miller's running to us from the big glass doors under the arches. Somebody snitched.

Kara, the middle school secretary, dropped out of community college when she got pregnant by her English professor. She moved back in with her mom and dad, across the street from Grandma and Grandpa's, when little Katy was born. Everybody always says she looks just as good now as before the baby. She has perky tits and a movie-star ass. Her pink lipstick, blue cat-eyes and braided light-brown hair almost make me forget about my sore jaw and knuckles. Kara smiles at me, then opens a black filing cabinet.

"Sorry about your grandpa," she says.

We would've buried Grandpa last week but they never found the body. Everybody's giving up on him, though. Uncle Ray says they probably dumped him in Lake Superior cause "that lake don't give up her dead." Dad thinks his body's somewhere in Canada, up by Wawa, where he went hunting with Lester Cronin. Grandma doesn't say much about any of it. I think she's afraid Grandpa just might come back.

The old mahogany clock ticks slow and cruel. Kara's making copies with her back turned to me. I should be worried about the trouble I'm in, but I can't stop staring at those legs—she's wearing black panty hose and a short black skirt— keeps bending over to give me a look. Then she catches me stare too long. First, she kind of smiles, but her mouth sours.

"What's the matter with you lately, Buck? It's the second time you've been here this week."

It's really the third time but I won't admit that. I'm not going to tell her why I'm really here either. Wouldn't do any good anyway. I want to tell her that I'm the good guy here. That Blake and Jay and Chris all ganged up on Malcolm, the slow kid whose mom sews mittens to his jacket sleeves. That they kicked him around and stole his money. I want to tell her that Chris and Blake kept slapping him in his face until he cried, even after they got his money. I want to tell Kara that they called him a pussy and a fag and a fucktard, trying to get him to fight, but Malcolm doesn't have a mean bone in him and wouldn't fight back. I won't tell her that I stood there watching all of this because these guys are supposed to be my friends but I might tell her that Blake took it too far when he sucker-punched Malcolm in the nose. It felt good to hit Blake, not just for Malcolm, but because Blake's had it coming for a long time. All I tell Kara is, "I don't know." She makes a face like she's ragging and goes back to copying.

I wish Grandpa could've been there to see me take down Blake. I never really got a good chance to make him proud of me. Now he's gone and he'll never know. Since there was no body, they had a picture of Grandpa on a folding table at the memorial. He was wearing a suit and tie, his hair slicked back. I've never seen him look more uncomfortable. Wonder where the hell they found that picture. He never dressed like that, except for Christmas mass. Everybody got up to say nice things about him at the memorial, even the people who didn't like him much. Death brings out everybody's best lies.

Kara's on the phone now and she points to Principal Roth's door, making that C-shaped sign with her thumb and finger. I know she means it's almost time to go in, but I can't help laugh, thinking she's telling me that Principal Roth's got a tiny dick. She would probably know. She gives me another look, like I'm crazy. Blake comes out half-crying. He whispers over to me that he's going to fucking kill me and says I'm a traitor. I tell him that at least I'm not a pussy who beats up retards. Kara looks over at us and Blake just smiles.

"Get back to class," she tells him. "And you—in there."

Principal Roth sits behind his varnished oak desk, legs crossed, in his leather swivel chair. He's on the phone but points me into a black plastic chair and shoots me a bad look. The white walls are covered with trout and bass mounts. He's even got a swordfish on the side wall next to Kara's office. His desk is piled high with neat stacks of files and paper and there's a couple copies of Field and Stream open on top of the stacks. When he hangs up, he catches me staring at a black and white picture with three guys in fancy fishing gear.

"You know who that guy on the left is? Ernest Hemingway. Caught that mess right there on the Fox River. Good looking feller there in the middle's yours truly. You fish, Buck? Rest of your family does."

"Yessir. You friends with Hemingway?"

"Hemingway's dead. What we going to do with you, Buck?

I'll tell you, you popped that Blake pretty damn good. You know I can't have fighting like that on school grounds, son."

There's a knock at the door and Kara comes in with a note. Principal Roth rolls his eyes and she shrugs back at him before she goes back out without looking my direction.

"Buck, your family's been through a lot with your grandpa and all, and I'm really sorry about that. He was a good man. I don't want to call your old man. He's got enough on his mind right now."

"Thank you, Mr. Roth."

"Now hold on there son. You can't just go around starting fights. Lunch detention, two weeks, just like that Braune boy. If you ever do this again, you little sombitch, I'll take you out back and give you ten times what you give Blake."

"I won't."

"Damn straight. Your grades are good enough, son. All's I'm saying is don't fuck it up."

Mrs. Gurov's Art class is the last period of the day. We're painting some stupid red flowers in a black pot. "Realism," she calls it. Katherine Beckett sits next to me, painting away, all serious. When I ask Katherine what time it is, she looks at my painting and says, "Not bad. If you put some effort into it, you could be good."

"No way. This is boring."

"How can you say that? I love this class."

"Maybe if we could paint something else."

Katherine smiles and sighs, like she feels sorry for me, but I can tell she wants to laugh. She lives in a red-brick house and has a lawyer for a dad, but she's not the snob some people think she is.

I try to think up something smart to tell her but the end-of-school bell rings.

Ronnie LeVasseur waves from across the street. Ronnie failed the sixth grade twice. He hangs out with all the kids that smoke by the big rock across from school. When I turn straight to walk down the hill from school to Uncle Eddie's house, he starts yelling, "Buck, get your ass over here." I don't usually hang out with most of these guys. I tried smoking cigarettes a few times with Uncle Tony and cigars with Blake and Chris but it didn't do much for me. Smoking's what this group is all about.

Ronnie's alright. He gave me a ride home a couple of times when it was so cold your piss would freeze before it hit the ground. He's sixteen already. Got a driver's license and a car, a brown '71 Oldsmobile. I don't like some of his friends though. Carl's got that crazy eye and Bobby's got a twitch. Me and some of the guys from the baseball team seen them two drinking gas behind the Standard station last summer when we were walking back from practice. They were with some other tall, skinny, curly-haired kid we don't know. They had a milk jug with about fifty cents worth of gas they must've got straight from the unleaded pump. They're all staring over at me now, but I walk over anyway cause I got to hear what Ronnie has to say.

"You ain't as much a pussy's I thought you was," Ronnie says. "You should've seen this guy bust fucking Blake Braune's nose."

"I hate that Blake cocksucker," Carl says. He's puffing a Marlboro Red and his gray eyes are glazed over.

"Me and Jason's thinking about going to Bay City Lake. Do some donuts on the ice. Wanna go?"

Everybody used to camp up at Bay City Lake in the summer till they found the body. Now it's mostly tourists come out there in the summer with their tents and campers. They don't know any better. They say it was Principal Roth found the body, all puffed-up and rotten. He was duck hunting out there in a camouflage rowboat when the stink hit him. First he thought it might be a bear. It was a little foggy in the dusk so he rowed around looking for the smell. One of his oars hit the body, Mr. Stash. Roth netted him and rowed him to the south shore landing. He drove in to town and called the cops from the store in Hessel.

Old Johnny Stash had been missing a few weeks. Last anyone heard from him, he was fighting with Brandon Jones over twenty dollars. Brandon did some work around the house for old man Stash. Stash said he did it half-ass and wasn't going to pay him. Next time anyone saw him, he was floating face-down in Bay City Lake with a .22 hole between his eyes. That put Roth in a rough spot cause the cops were trying to figure out what happened and started to ask him all kinds of questions. Came out that he was with a woman when he found Stash. She wasn't his wife. Her story kept him innocent from murder but took him straight to a divorce. Cops figured out later it was Brandon Jones who done it. Broke into Stash's house and killed him. Brandon was drunk and high, like always, and went to get his money—maybe a little extra—out of the Folger's can where Stash kept his poker money. They found Brandon's greedy fingerprints on the coffee can. Just dumped it on the floor and ran with the cash. Since then, they boarded up the windows of Stash's tar-paper shack and hardly nobody goes out to Bay City Lake. This is a dare from Ronnie, so I go.

We stop by the Rez to get some gas money. Ronnie's Uncle Bear smokes a brass pipe outside the door of his house. The outside walls are half-finished, with tar-paper dangling by the windows. Water drips from the saw-tooth shaped icicles that hang from the underside of his A-frame roof. Slush wets the deck under Bear's feet.

"Hey Bear, spot me a J," Ronnie says.

"I ain't got no more," says Bear.

"Bullshit. Linda said you bought an eighth last night from Mikey."

"It's only a eighth, Ronnie. I can't get no more till next week."

"You didn't waste it already?"

"You boys can have a puff. Just don't get greedy."

First Bear passes it to Ronnie, then Ronnie gives it to Jason.

"You don't have to, Buck."

"No, it's cool," I tell him.

"That's it. Toke it up boy," says Bear.

It's my first time smoking weed. I know the smell. Dad and Uncle Tony smoke it all the time. I'm just starting to get a little buzz when Bear wipes the bowl with his black sweater and puts the pipe in his jean pocket. We go into Ronnie's house for bread and peanut butter. "Stairway to Heaven" is on the black and silver turntable.

"This song's about getting high," Jason says.

"No it ain't," says Ronnie. "It's about religion and spirituality and shit like that."

"You're both right," says Bear.

Ronnie grabs a half loaf of bread and a Ziploc bag full of change from the counter to get gas in Hessel. There's no peanut butter. Before we walk out the door, I see the picture of Ronnie's little brother, Cody. Was almost a year ago now he drowned. Ronnie grabs a half pouch of Beechnut on the way out the door and makes the sign of the cross toward Cody's picture before he steps out and locks up.

On the way into town, we pass Anna James and Beth Cortes walking up the hill by the Baptist church. Bear and Jason are in the back seat and they tell Ronnie to roll down the window.

"You beautiful ladies need a ride," says Bear. "Plenty of room back here."

"No thanks," says Beth.

"It's cold out there," Bear says. "Come on inside and I'll warm you up."

"Gross. Go away," Anna says.

We're all laughing until Anna looks over at me.

"Really, Buck? I would expect better from you."

"Let's get going," says Ronnie. "We got more important shit to do than dick around here."

He peels out and the tires from the Oldsmobile spray black slush and snow on Beth's jeans and boots.

"Stuck up bitches," says Bear. "Who needs 'em."

"I do," says Jason. "I'm tired of jerking off all the time."

"I'd show them girls something," Bear says.

"You realize that's illegal, Bear," says Ronnie. "They're only like twelve or thirteen. You're what, forty."

"Thirty-nine. Back in the old days, none of that mattered. Your great grandma was twelve when she married my grandpa. He was fifty. That was normal."

"Bullshit," says Ronnie. "That was never normal."

"Don't question the wisdom of your elders, you worthless little fuck," says Bear.

"Be a good elder and make yourself useful," says Ronnie. "Get us a fifth of Schnapps."

The Oldsmobile slides to a stop next to the only gas pump in Hessel. Ronnie's black rosary swings back and forth from the rearview mirror, tapping the glass of the windshield three times. The rosary reminds me of the one Great Grandma Marie used to wear.

She was always reading the Bible. Went to mass at least four times a week until she got real sick from diabetes. When I was six, she told me this Bible story about a kid named Joseph. His older brothers sold him to slavery cause they were jealous of him. He went through a bunch of shit but he ended-up being a king or something. Great Grandma Marie always said that when people pick on people like that, it's because they're jealous. Used to think this might be true. Blake wasn't jealous when he sucker-punched Malcolm, though. Only reason Blake did it he's a fucking prick. Nobody wants to be Malcolm. Malcolm ain't never going to get rich and shame people like Blake for what they did. Put Blake up against Malcolm a million times, and a million times, Blake wins.

Ronnie is counting up the change. There's almost three dollars in the plastic bag. Bear passes up two dollars from the back seat. Jason's got eighty-six cents. I give Ronnie the buck-fifty I got.

"Here's the plan. We need some booze, some food and some gas," says Ronnie.

"We ain't got enough for everything," says Bear.

"You get us the bottle. Something cheap. What's left over for gas. Jay, you take care of the food. Buck and I'll keep old lady Eunice busy. Should be just the two of them."

The air's getting colder and the sun's going down. The streetlight in front of the store stutters on and we walk through the door, making the bell ring. There's only one person working, Eunice Murphy. She's stocking cigarettes behind the counter, her silver-black braid swinging side to side. She turns to us and pushes her brown circle frames farther up the bridge of her nose with her ring finger. Her black dress with red flower print covers most of her short pudgy body.

"Looks like trouble," she says.

Bear laughs, but she doesn't. "What's good in the liquor cabnet," he asks her.

"You wouldn't be buying nothing for these boys, would you? You know I can't do that."

"Hell no. Ronnie just give me a ride into town. Needed to get some gas. I needs to get me some fuel myself, know what I mean."

He laughs again and she looks at him serious. It's so quiet when Bear stops laughing, you can really hear the old floorboards creak under Jason's feet while he walks the third aisle, scoping things out.

"Them boys gonna have to leave if I sell you liquor. Wouldn't look right."

Bear nods to the door. Ronnie looks over to Jason. Tells him to hurry. Old Eunice is climbing the step ladder, reaching for bottles when the bell clanks against the glass door. Jason's the last one of the three of us out the door. He bumps his head on the plywood windbreaker around the outside frame of the glass door and almost slips on an ice patch. Ronnie and I jump in the front of the Oldsmobile and Jason in the back.

"Start this fucker up. It's cold," Jason says.

"Got to save gas," says Ronnie. "What you get? Let's see it."

"I got some shit. Just wait a minute."

"Let's get away from here first," I say.

Bear comes out with a little brown paper bag. His eyes are bloodshot and his long black hair blows loose in the wind. He gets in the back and pulls out a glass bottle of Peppermint Schnapps.

"That's a fucking pint," Ronnie says. "I told you get a fifth."

"Wasn't enough left," says Bear.

"Left?"

"Had to get a pack of Marlboro Lights and some Zig-Zags."

"Motherfucker. How much left for gas, Uncle Bernard?"

"Don't call me that you little shit."

"How much?"

"Sixty-eight cents."

"Won't get too far on that. Buck, get out there and pump it. Too cold for me."

I never pumped gas before. Seen people do it and it looks easy enough.

"Pull the metal lever back," says Ronnie. "Towards the car."

I get it to sixty-five cents and try to slow it down but every time I click and let go, it goes up two cents. The dial rolls past sixty-nine, to seventy, by the time I get it to stop.

"Just get in," Bear says. As soon as I do, Ronnie peels out around the corner, the back tires of the Oldsmobile skidding toward the frozen parking lot of the marina. The sunset is red and gray over Hessel Bay.

Before my cousin Joe went to the Army, he told me a story about how he was coming back from a party in St. Ignace with Allen Terry and Big Todd when they were high school juniors. They lost a basketball game against Brimley, but they usually lost, so it wasn't a big deal. Allen's cousin Mark worked at the waterfront IGA in downtown St. Ignace. They picked him up after work so he could get some beer. Mark said there was a party on First Street so they all hung out there for a while. It was mostly a sausage party, so they dropped off Mark at about 11:00, after they picked up another case.

They took Old St. Ignace Road back to Hessel so they could drink with less chance of running into cops. When they got to Three Mile Road, they turned north to drop off Big Todd. They were passing the airport and Allen dared Joe to take his gray Mustang out to Bay City Lake. Big Todd told Joe he didn't have the balls. Joe slid the Mustang into the left turn and drove it in.

They got as far as the field by the south side of the lake and started doing donuts. Really tore up the ice. So much they almost got stuck before they finished off the case of Old Milwaukee. They sat out by the open ice for a while, then Allen told Joe to take the car up the hill to the backroads around the lake. Joe knew the car wouldn't make it, but he was drunk enough to try. Besides, he didn't want to go home to my uncle and aunt as drunk as he was. Big Todd and Allen said they'd push if he got stuck. They didn't make it more than a quarter mile up the road from the field, and they skidded sideways into a snow bank. Spent the rest of the night digging and pushing. By the time they got the Mustang turned around and headed back out, it was morning, and they were running on fumes. They saw people lining up for the dogsled race when they hit Three Mile Road again. Drove right past a state trooper. By that time, didn't matter—they were sober as the sled dogs.

We don't have enough gas to drive up to Bay City Lake and spin out on the ice, so Ronnie, Jason, Bear and me just drive around Hessel, out to the point, and then we take a backroad to Cedarville. Probably better that way anyway. Don't think any of us are up for pushing the Oldsmobile out of the ditch if we get stuck up there. It's way too fucking cold, even with the heater on. Jason passes around the bag of cheese puffs he stole from the store. He pulls out some Topps baseball cards and a few cans of sardines.

"Nice job, dipshit," says Ronnie. "You could've stoled something good. These ain't even real Cheetos."

"If you don't want 'em, I'll take yours," I say.

"Give me some of them baseball cards," says Ronnie.

Bear lights a cigarette. We drive out around Hill Island, passing around the Schnapps till it's gone. Doesn't take long the way Bear slugs it down. I get the last shot.

"Backwash," Ronnie says. "Toss it out the window."

It's about eight thirty when Ronnie drops me off. Mom's car and Dad's truck are both in the driveway. The kitchen light is on. I try to be cool walking in so they won't notice my buzz. When I open the door, nobody's there, just half a fifth of Canadian Mist on the kitchen counter and an empty shot glass. I check the bedrooms. Nobody's anywhere around. I get a towel from the bathroom and wash up. I brush my teeth. I feel the three packs of baseball cards Jason gave me in my upper left coat pocket. Never stole anything before. Guess I didn't technically steal anything today either, but it still feels wrong. I think of the cheese balls and start to gag. Choke up puffy orange chunks into the sink, so I take a swig of Listerine and roll it around in my mouth. I swallow a little mouthwash before I can spit it into the sink. When the bathroom door opens behind me, the last of the yellow-orange foam swirls down the drain.

"Where you been?" Dad asks. He's in Carhart overalls and red rubber boots, yellow jersey gloves hanging out his back pocket. "Pass me the mouthwash. Got called in to work some O.T. Midnight shift."

"Where's mom?"

"She took your brothers over to Ma's. Virginia picked 'em up. Some paperwork and shit cause of your grandpa. Should be back any time now."

"You okay to drive to work?"

"Might want to change your shirt before the old lady gets home. Smells like smoke."

"Wasn't me. Some of the guys in Ronnie's car. Not me."

"Shouldn't do that shit. I ever tell you about my old man catching me with a cigar?"

"You told me."

"That's how they did it in the old days. I'm gonna miss that crazy old bastard. He wasn't all bad, you know." I nod until I can't keep my head from tilting down. "You might want to just take a shower. Smell you from two miles away."

He walks out and I look in the mirror. My eyes are bloodshot and I notice my own stink now. When Dad was a kid, Grandpa caught him smoking. Made Dad smoke a pack of cigarettes while he beat him with a cedar switch. Grandpa bent Dad over a stump with his pants down and just beat Dad's ass till he was too tired to lift his arm. My old man yelled out the first couple times but never cried. Kept smoking till the whole pack was gone. Neither one said a word to each other for a whole year after that.

If I get in the shower now, I might make it to bed before Mom gets home.

It's Valentine's Day and Malcolm hands me a card in the hall. It has a pink heart on the cover and on the inside it says, "I love you, Buck. I'm glad you're my friend." Anna James grabs it from me and laughs. Then she runs over to Katherine to show her. Katherine rolls her eyes. Got to stop this before it goes too far. I walk over and grab the card back, rip it up and throw it in the black plastic trash bin. Malcolm stares at me, smiling by the white ceramic fountain. I grab his shoulder and tell him, "You got to stop doing things like this. If you tell me you love me and give me Valentine's Day cards, people are going to call us fags. Don't you get that?"

"What's a fag, Buck?"

"Never mind. Just stop giving me things."

"But I want to give you things. You're my best friend."

"No, I'm not Malcolm. We can't be friends. Don't you get that."

"Why not? I love you because you helped me. Nobody helps me like you, Buck."

"I'm not your friend. I can't even look out for myself."

"It's okay. We can be fags. I don't care," he tells me.

I'm sure he doesn't know what he's saying, but I can't stop my fist from punishing his chin. It's like somebody else took over my body and we're on the floor, my knee on his chest. Malcolm tries to wiggle away. I push his head down with my palm, making it bounce on the red concrete tiles like a basketball every time he tries to pick it up. I stop and look around. Nobody's laughing anymore.

Malcolm covers his face with both hands. He's crying, his eyes swelling behind his thick, black-taped, brown frames. I get up and slam my fist into Anna's locker. Everybody's staring now. Some are laughing again. Maybe at me. Maybe at Malcolm. Somebody yells, "Psycho." Blake has a shit-eating grin. Before he can make a smart ass comment, I tell him, "Don't make me kick your ass again." The bell for seventh hour rings. I'm walking away when Blake yells, "Whenever you wanna go, we can take it outside, pussy. You can bring your fagtard for backup when you guys kiss and make up."

We're back to painting in Mrs. Gurov's seventh hour Art class. My flowers aren't as good as I thought they were yesterday. They got red lines running from the petals into the stems and the potted black dirt looks like roof tar. I painted some spots darker than others for no good reason and there's open white spaces where there shouldn't be. When we're finished painting the red flowers, we'll move on to some other bullshit project. Doesn't really matter. I turn to Katherine Beckett. "I get this Realism," I tell her. I'm still sweating and shaking a little, even though I tried to clean up with brown paper towel in the restroom.

"Nice for you, Buck," she says.

Just when I'm about to tell her something smart, something that would've made her laugh yesterday—something "charming," like she says—she turns to the window and the red, potted flowers. I notice something about her painting: it's almost perfect. I could never be that patient.

Sixth period I left a Valentine for Katherine in her locker. No way she's seen it yet. Told her everything—how beautiful I thought she was—how smart and classy and kind. Wonder if there's time to get it back before she gets to her locker.

Dad got a side job fixing up summer cabins. When Mr. Roth called him about Malcolm, he told me I'd be helping him out after school for a couple weeks. Mostly repairs and some grunt work, nothing too hard, but it's cold cause they shut off the power till May. At least these are Fisher's cabins, not Braune's, so I won't have to hear any shit from Blake at school.

"Get the putty," Dad says. He's showing me how to fix leaks. Couple pipes broke with the freeze last night. Our hands and sleeves are wet from the pipe. Dad's coat's full of soot and his face is orange and brown from plumbing rust.

"How much you make here?" I ask him.

"Not so good, but Fisher says any booze still laying round's mine." He takes a pint of Root Beer Schnapps out his back pocket for a swig, then hands it to me. "It's okay. Take a pull," he says. The pipe stops dripping. Dad sets down his tools and motions me outside.

He grabs a milk jug of gas from by the cabin door and walks out by the dock. He pours most the jug on a pile of scrapwood and garbage bags, then lights it up with a rolled-up piece of newspaper.

"Bring that rocker over here," he says. "Throw it in."

It's nightfall—that late winter kind, and a light breeze from Lake Huron blows the birch branches just enough to make a smooth rocking noise. There's music from the chimes on the main cabin. Dad looks calmer than I've seen him for a while, warming his gloves over the junk fire.

"How them fingers?" He asks. "Some places it never gets this cold. Spent all winter down in Georgia one year. Got cold but nothing like this."

"Never knew you lived in Georgia."

"Basic Training and Ranger School. You know there's no sweets in Basic Training? Don't stop some people though. This guy—we called him Candyman—he was always after the sweets. Stole cake and pie from the NCOs for some time till they wised up to it."

Dad passes me the bottle for another swig. Never seen him drink Root Beer Schnapps before but he always says any liquor's good liquor, especially free liquor. There's a crunch in the woods behind a smaller cabin. We stop a few minutes to listen but don't hear it again.

"Faun, maybe," Dad says. "One time they call us down to formation, two-thirty in the AM. Caught Candyman stealing cake from a West Point cadet. They send infantry cadets to train at Benning in the summer. We was all pissed off cause you hardly get sleep as it is. Whole battalion stood at attention while they smoked the Candyman. Then they smoked us."

"Why? You didn't do it."

"The way it is, Son. The brotherhood—everybody pays for the sins of the one. Fair or not."

"That's bullshit."

"Maybe, but that's that. After they smoked us, twenty-five mile road march in full gear. Candyman sat his ass back at the barracks and ate cake."

"What happened to Candyman?"

"He got processed out. But that night he got it good. Worse than a blanket party. Couple guys held him in his bunk while the whole platoon give him a beating. Even took metal shine boxes to his legs and back. Rammed a Snickers bar up his ass and told him, "Here you go Candyman. How you like your candy now?"

"Did you get him too?"

"Never forget that look Candyman gave me the next day in the latrine. He was a skinny little shit with birth control glasses. But there he was, judge and jury, beady-eyed little sombitch. Thought I had it figured out till I saw that look. Now I don't know what to make of anything really."

It's clear over Government Bay and the stars light up the black space over the lake and trees. We have a couple shelves and window frames to tend while the junk fire smolders down, so we go to the truck for a level and tape. In the truck light, I see my clothes are as orange and rusty as Dad's and the smoke stink might be a two-shower job. Dad tries to find a good station on his portable AM, but there's no music, just talk. Snowmobiles rev it up on the bay. Their lights point out to Big LaSalle Island.

1994

Red lights flash from below the hill, signals that they're our guys. Not just any blue helmets, Americans.

"Must be Hansen," Stubbs says.

"Just here yesterday. Why's he back already? Maybe we're going back to our units," says Perry.

"'Bout damn time," Wiggins says. "I'm sick of y'all infantry motherfuckers and your camping out. All that damn digging. Thought it was bad in my unit."

"Wouldn't get my hopes up just yet, wigger," says Stubbs. "And I told you to watch your fucking mouth when higher brass comes around. It's just damn disrespectful."

Hansen's with two young guys, privates. Looks like they're fresh out of basic, their uniforms clean and new. Hansen's BDUs are faded but he's clean-shaved and he looks showered, from what I can see in the flashlights.

"There's a rogue set up shop on a hill two clicks from here. Over yonder hill, right up from that UN re-supply hub, one the Swedes are running. Doesn't know we're here behind him. Might be a sniper or calling in mortars. My boys here, Mendoza and Cooper, been watching him through the green light. They said y'all had the sniper rifle."

"Got the rifle, but no sniper," says Stubb.

"Nothing but clerks and jerks in my attachment," Hansen says. "Let's get a team of your boys on that ridge. Set one of 'em up about a half click out and pop that sombitch first daylight. I'd do it but my eyes ain't what they used to."

"How 'bout you, Robinson," Perry says, "want to take down a white boy?

"No Sarge, you know it never work out well, black man shoots a white man. Never been nothing but trouble for my people."

"I'll do it," says Wiggins. "Give that pavlaka-eating motherfucker a taste of Oakland."

"Sniper rifle takes a little more skill than a drive-by, son. What y'all need is a bonafied backwoods, deer-hunting country boy," says Stubb.

"Van Dorn's country. Mississippi boy," says Perry.

"It'll be just like deer season," Stubb says.

"I'm from Jackson, Sir," Van Dorn tells him. "My old man's a dentist. Never did much hunting. Nobody else wants to do it, I'll give it my best, Sir."

"How 'bout you, Metzger? You's kind of backwoods," Perry says.

"And he's one of our boys, 11B. Ever take down a buck Metzger?" Stubb asks me while he lights his cigarette.

"Every year since I was nine," I tell him. "Till I joined the Army."

"Can you take down an objective at 500 meters? Probably shot bucks from a couple hundred with a 30.06? Sniper rifle's same difference."

"Yessir."

"I'd get that motherfucker real good," says Wiggins. "Give me that gun. I want to get me some action. Sarge Metzger don't even want no action. Just told us all so."

"Last thing we need's a lot of noise," says Major Hansen.

"Don't need an international incident. Wiggins running in like Wyatt Earp, shooting shit up. Maybe you should stay back on this one," says Stubb.

"Hell no. I ain't gonna miss this. Metzger choke, I'll run in there and give that Euro-cracker a beatdown."

"Good, you're Metzger's spotter. One shot, one kill, boy," he tells me. "You miss, the shit goes down."

"I won't," I tell him. I won't.

"Well hot damn. We got ourselves a sniper," says Major Hansen.

"Even better, a redneck grunt with a deer rifle," says Perry. "I'm getting a hard-on already."

Perry hands me the black plastic case.

"You can do this, son," says Hansen. He slaps me hard on the back.

I pull the rifle out of the case and wipe it down. Make sure it's not loaded and run the ramrod in to clear debris. It's not all that dirty on the inside compared to how dusty it was on the outside. I've never fired this exact rifle but it's really not too different from some of our hunting rifles back home.

First buck I shot was a five point. Dad was with me and his hands were shaking when he handed me the 30.06. I wasn't nervous at all. Too young to know the difference. Just aimed—lined up the deer in the scope and squeezed the trigger once I got a clear steady picture through the glass. Dropped that deer right over the pile of brown apples Dad left for bait. He was screaming, excited when we went to drag it back through the woods. It was so heavy, awkward and dead, snapping twigs and leaving a blood trail in the crisp snow. It's one thing with a deer, another with a human, and with humans, there's usually not this much time to think about it.

We set up on the closest ridge and watched the Bosnian through the green light of night vision for a few minutes but he bedded down behind some rocks before we could get a clear shot. Perry thought about sneaking up on him, but if he woke, he'd have the advantage up on the hill and there's a good chance he'd hear us. Before basic training, I never fired at a human silouhette, the kind of targets they use downrange to train soldiers. Shooting at the black silouhettes is a strange enough feeling, but then they got the ones that look like real people, the ones in the bright green uniforms. I missed my first few shots at qualifications just because it weirded me out so much firing at the little green men. Cost me expert. Then I started thinking about Lester Cronin. Ever since then, every time I fire the M-16, the M-60, AT-4, M 203 grenade launchers, 50 cal, the SAW, or whatever, it's always Cronin at the other end.

The man through the binoculars doesn't look like Cronin though. He stirs again for the first time just as the sun's coming up from the valley over the pink sky. The Bosnian wears a kind of camouflage more like what we might wear back home during deer season. He takes off his cap and scratches his light brown hair and

I see that he's young, no older than twenty or so. He never turns completely toward us but he looks down at the UN camp through a sort of telescope and I see the side of his face. For a minute, he smiles, maybe laughs, like he's thinking of a private joke. Then he writes notes in a black ledger. Something about him reminds me a little of me.

Morgan's clumsy with the tripod.

"Let's set this shit up," he tells me. "Hurry up or I'm taking that rifle."

"I don't need a tripod," I tell him.

"Don't be stupid," says Perry. "You need support. If you miss this, we're all toast. Those Swedes will call down the fucking rain on these hills."

"Never shot with a tripod. With all due respect, Top, back off and let me get this."

"You miss, your ass is running down to draw him out."

Last night, Major Hansen said that this is for the good of everybody. That I can save a lot of spilled blood this way. No telling what the guy on the hill is up to. They say the snipers in Sarajevo take out women and children and brag about it to their friends—count everything on their kill lists. I kept looking through the binoculars, trying to find a sniper rifle, a pistol, some kind of weapon to make it all easier to justify snuffing him out. Wiggins and Perry stare at me and Perry whispers for me to hurry. It's not my job to think, they both tell me.

"Don't miss. Come on, man, you got this." It's the first time I've seen Sergeant Perry so nervous, excited about anything here.

"Smoke that mo'fucka," Wiggins tells me.

I rest my left arm on top of a bushel-basket-sized rock and rest the barrel on my left hand. Then I take a breath and lean in to the scope to line up the crosshairs. I move my head forward till the circle in the scope fills with a picture of where the sky meets hilltop. The Bosnian, whatever his gang is, gives me a wide target with his back toward the crosshairs. Just like a deer, I could miss by half a foot and drop him with a long shot. He'd choke to death on his own blood while he suffocated, holding the bloody hole with his hands. It's a hell of a state to put an animal in, worse a man. If I pull, a single round will snuff out the problem and the Bosnian won't be in any shape to call back-up or artillery. He'll drop and it'll be hours before his unit figures it out, if not days. He's probably radio silent with so many damn factions out here. I should just drop him, do my duty. I hear Wiggins' and Perry's heartbeats and their exhales heavy around me—sometimes I can't tell if it's me or them, the three of us sweating in unison. I feel my chest move and it makes the image in the scope bounce from the man's waist to the air over his shoulder. I could never shoot a man in the back, unless that man's Lester Cronin. So I start to squeeze and think of Lester Cronin but the Bosnian bounces around in my scope again. I steady my breath and he turns to the side, giving me centimeters for a margin of error. He faces our position and might see my head and the rifle barrel, so I squeeze the trigger. The Bosnian stumbles in my scope and drops.

1984

In mid-April the bank that leads up to the mouth of the Carp River is a five-mile stretch of shantytown. Whiskey and beer bottles everywhere, the Carp curves and cuts its way through pine, sand and birch into Lake Huron. Bonfires and frosted taillights mark the way down the dusty path over mud ruts and maple roots. Old men sit smoking on rusted-out tailgates, bologna sandwiches in the cooler, booze at the ready. Kids slosh through sand and clay in pint-sized hip-waders that stretch to their necks. The dippers' nets shine in our headlights when the trail curves the truck toward the water. Dad steers down the campsite road that shadows the river and Uncle Tony tokes up from the passenger side.

"Boys hungry?" Dad tosses back a greasy paper bag with venison and butter sandwiches.

Me, Johnny, Tommy and Cousin Ryan ride back in the Ford's wood truck bed. Dad rigged the wood frame up and bolted it in when the metal one rusted out. It's painted blue to match the cab, but you can tell it's not a pro job.

Johnny peels most of the napkin from the sandwich. "My bread's all wet," he says.

I take a bite and get a mouthful of napkin. Don't say a word, just spit it out.

"You boys wouldn't make it in the Army," Dad says. He stops for a second to sip his Old Milwaukee. "You don't even imagine some of the shit we ate there, right Tony."

Dad slides the rear glass window open all the way and holds out his hand. Styx plays on the eight track. The smoky mist drifts up through the night pines. Ryan coughs. I'm sitting on the cooler so I slide back, pop the lid, and pass a couple Old Milwaukees in to Uncle Tony and Dad.

"What's the worst thing you ate," I ask him.

"Bugs, rats, piss," says Uncle Tony. "Hell, your old man even ate a shit sandwich one time, right Gene."

"We ate shit sandwich every day back in the bush." Dad's eyes shift back and forth from the road to the rearview mirror.

Tony looks like the devil with the red glow from the cab around his slick, black hair. Smoke circles hang over his bulletproof cheeks and handlebar moustache. They must've been talking about Grandpa again, cause they got that dead quiet look. Then Tony says, "Pass up a couple three more. Gonna two-fist it." It's more than five months now since Grandpa disappeared, but none of us can forget what happened. Dad says he and Uncle Jack got a plan. Says they'll bring in Uncle Tony. Dad and Tony got more spare time now. Both of 'em laid off from the boats. Old Lester Cronin's gonna get his payback. Dad and Tony were Rangers in the Army.

Dad and Tony don't know it, but I heard Uncle Jack, Dad's baby brother, tell Colonel Henry the Pete Girard story last night. When Dad first came back from Vietnam, he found out his sister, Aunt Karen, got pregnant. Grandma told Dad it was a rape, but not to tell Grandpa. The family was waiting for Dad to get home to help take care of Pete. That's when Tony first came up from Texas. Karen kept crying until Dad got the truth out of her. Girard got drunk and forced her. Choked her pretty little neck with his left hand while he fucked her mean. Karen didn't want Dad to hurt Pete cause he was her boyfriend right up to the day before, until she found out about Pete's wife in Columbus. Dad told Aunt Karen none of that mattered once Pete did what he did.

Pete Girard didn't know Dad or Tony from any other locals. His family always came up in the summer from Ohio since he was a kid, but the only Metzger he knew was Aunt Karen. Jack told Henry it was easy for Dad and Tony to get Pete out to the Carp to dip smelt. They smoked a few joints with Pete behind Cronin's Hardware and sealed the deal. Jack rode out to the river with him, in the back of Tony's Dodge. Says Pete was a cocky drunk—bragged the whole trip out that he didn't have to work cause he lived off his old man's money—tire business down in Ohio. He told Jack he was gonna trip acid when he got out to the Carp. Make it all psychodelic. Pete wasn't much for fishing.

Neither Jack or Pete saw it coming. Jack went to sleep around midnight and he woke up to the scream. Saw Tony toss something red into a five gallon bucket of smelt. Dad was on top of Pete, holding his right arm down, knee in the small of Pete's back. Tony was holding a bloody Buck knife and kicking clumps of ground and dust into Pete's face. Jack heard Dad say, "Guess what's next?" Jack walked over to Tony, asked him what was going on. Saw Pete's hand in the bucket. Dad told Jack, "Go for a walk, you ain't seen nothing. Empty that bucket of smelt while you're at it. It ain't no good no more." Jack dumped the bucket. Then he heard another splash come from behind him. Nobody saw Pete Girard around town after that. Nobody around here missed him.

When Jack got done telling Colonel Henry the story about Pete Girard, he was choked up, but Henry's face didn't change the whole time. All Henry did was puff his cigar and say, "Those're the stains of kin. Yessir—the binding stains of kin." Then Jack looked at me and told me to never tell anybody that story or he'd kill me.

The metallic blue Chevy in front of us pulls off to the left. Dad hits a rut and knocks the sandwich out of little Tommy's hand.

"What's it like to smoke them gooks," Johnny asks.

"I hope you never find out, boy," says Uncle Tony. Dad looks kind of sober all the sudden. He doesn't say anything, but he's thinking hard.

"What was it like," I ask him. "Vietnam."

"Different than you think," says Uncle Tony. "This one time we's walking through the jungle. Middle of fucking nowhere, and we hear this noise. Sounds like a baby, but there's nobody round, and we're humping through some hot terrain. We're thinking it's a goat but it's a real human fucking baby. Laying there in the paddy, by some plants—look like little palm trees. Sometimes, over there, you might think you're in Florida or Hawaii or some damned place, but for the bullets all round."

"A baby?" Ryan laughs.

"Sounds like bullshit to me," says Johnny.

"You wanna hear the story or not," says Tony. "Platoon Sergeant says to leave it, keep going. Lieutenant Boyle says, 'Don't touch it. Might be a booby trap.' What kind of shit is that? Strapping grenades to babies. But these V.C. don't fuck around. Do whatever it takes. We saw the kind of crazy nobody believe—less you were there."

Tony cracks another Old Milwaukee.

There's nowhere good left to park at the river mouth, so Dad circles around back to the north side road, over where the sand bar splits the river. When he finds a spot, we all hop out where the tail-gate should be while the Ford jumps and sputters dead, headlights aimed at the river bank. Johnny and I run over to the hard sandy ledge, trying to get a look at the river. It's six feet down—can't see much. The water, coffee and milk color, runs fast till it empties in St. Martin's Bay. The headlights and spotlights all around make it hard to see anything but the steel mesh and poles of the smelt nets. The current crackles loud over old men's bullshit and the C.C.R. that whines through AM radio. The wind rips through hard every few minutes, then calms. I snatch the net away from my little brother Tommy, walk the trail down to the water and start to dip. Can't tell if Tommy's gonna cry or he's just shivering up there in his blue hood. Green and yellow snot leaks from both sides of his red nose. Everything smells like fish, cedar and smoke. I breathe it all in and step into the muck. The Carp's flow pulls me closer, almost takes me in. Dad anchors me. Must've followed me down. He pulls the collar of my ripped blue coat. Steadies me on the bank.

"This ain't too far from where that kid drown last year, eh Gene," says Uncle Tony from the trail. "Never found him till the next morning. One of the LeVasseur boys. Cory?"

"No, Cody," I say. "Ronnie's little brother."

"Cody. We was here when it happened, eh Gene. Took least a good six- pack afore his old man figured out he was missing. Suppose you kinda expect it with a family like that. Breed too much. So many little bastards running round there's no 'countability for 'em. Old man never heard of propalactics or what? So drunk he couldn't hardly walk too. Wasn't long, though, one of them boys was looking to take back the net from that little Cody or Cory. Old

LeVasseur 'bout shit himself when he seen the boy gone. Ended that party real quick."

"Had us all out here, shining the river with every light west of Drummond Island," Dad says. "About four in the morning, old man Jacques was down on his knees, crying to God in French. Was daylight by the time that Williams boy saw the red sweatshirt hung up on a root downriver, right that way."

"Half the town needed a jump start that morning," Tony says. "I was one of 'em. So caught up looking for the kid, my headlights was on all night. When the trooper come by, I told him I was good. You know me—I ain't getting help from no fucking pig. Had a quarter pound in my trunk. Almost got stuck out here cause of it—sweating it out till all the porkbellies split. Funny thing, it was LeVasseur himself who give me a jump. A rough shape that poor bastard was in."

"Did you see him, Uncle Tony," Johnny asks him.

"See who? The LeVasseur boy. Yep, we saw the body. Kid was bloated good, only a few hours in the river, right Gene?"

Dad nods. He's helping Tommy and Ryan dip with the other net. Looks like they're really catching 'em too. Dad shines the flashlight on the five-gallon bucket to show us. It's filling fast.

"You never told us what happened with the baby," Tommy says.

"The grenade," says Ryan.

"So I see it there. Muddy blanket stuck in a pile of jungle shit. Baby looked clean. Best I could tell, there's no wire. Big stupid bastard I am, I kneel down to it and tell the platoon to clear out. Sergeant Preston says, 'Step away from the baby.' Tells me, 'That's an order, Vega.' He's scared shitless, knows I won't listen to him, and he backs off with the rest of 'em, except your old man. Gene's down on the ground there with me, looking for wires under the baby. I remember we looked at each other, thinking we might be blowed to shit any second. Then I picked it up. Nothing—just stopped crying."

Tony stares out to the dark side of the trail, into the maples.

"Then what happened," I say. "Did he die?"

"Who?" Says Tony.

"In the Nam," I say.

"It was a girl," he says. "About then I got really scared. Started thinking what we was gonna do with it. Couldn't just leave it there. Boyle wanted to, but he was too churchy to order us not to take it. 'I ain't responsible for that damned thing,' he said. 'You wanna get your dick shot off for a little dink baby, that's your business. Dumbass grunts.' That Boyle was alright for a college boy. Your old man rigged up some bandage straps to sling that baby up on his shoulder."

That's as far as Tony gets in his story before he's got to take a piss. He walks out to the tree line with his Zippo and Zig-Zags.

Tomorrow's Good Friday. We got half a day of school, but most of us won't be there. I must've seen about half the guys in my class here—Chris, Jay and Paul and a few more. It's so dark, who knows who else is out there. I already got one turn with the hip waders. I was out there a good hour or more. The old man and I went to the shallows but it still was up to my thighs. After a while, you really start to feel the cold in the water, even with the waders. I got my gloves and winter coat on, but there's no way to keep your clothes dry when you're half a net deep in smelt. I can really feel the chill now, out of the water. Dipping works up a sweat, especially when they're running good. One pull, the net was so heavy, almost took me downstream. Dad was close by again, but even strong as he is, I wonder if he could've got me in time if I fell. "Keep your head up and your back straight, less you want to take a dip," he said. I filled the bucket myself a couple times, the catch shining like Coors Light cans in the headlights of the old Ford. When the five-gallon bucket filled again, it was Johnny's turn in the waders, so now I do the dumping. Three black trash bags sit almost full in the truckbed.

The music's quieter now that most the party crowd's gone. Only the serious dippers and drunks stick around this late. The slow breeze in from the bay is just cold enough to frost my neck and give me goosebumps on my arms. The spot on the river where we're at's got a tree on the other side, growing sideways out the bank. It swings back and forth real slow over the brown water like an old man in a rocking chair. It's not so crowded on the bank now that most the traffic's gone. Uncle Tony's still smoking with Chester Wolff out by the maples on the other side of the road. The moonlight's bright enough now I can see their faces. They're both real serious—probably talking about Lacey again. She left him on Christmas day and he still breaks down every time he talks about her. There's nothing like a six-foot-three 250 pound Italian-Mexican with a big bushy moustache, fifth of Popov in hand, rolling around in the dirt crying like a baby in his leather Harley jacket. When it happens, about once a week or so, Dad's quick to point out that even though Tony's like a brother, he's not blood.

Tommy and Ryan sleep in the cab of the pick-up. Their blanket is the canvass tarp strip Dad uses to cover his tools in the truck bed. Ryan's mouth is open like a smelt sucking for water. Tommy's curled up like a bear cub. Rest of the guys took a break from the river. Dad's chugging Old Milwaukee with my baseball coach, Mr. Roth. They're drunk laughing by the cooler in the back. Johnny plays catch with Roth's kid. His name's Johnny too. They're both fifth graders but the Roth kid's a fat little fuck. My brother Johnny's skinny like me. People always say we look like twins, but I'm taller, older.

Colonel Henry and Grandma Clio used to come out here every year, long as I can remember. Never showed up this year, though. They're not big into dipping smelt, but they sit around the fire, drink beer and smoke with the best of 'em. Last year they got here around one in the morning with some hot plates of pulled pork, mashed potatoes, brown beans and barbecue sauce. Must be five in the morning now and I'm starving. The venison sandwiches and can of brown beans we had are long gone now. There's a part of me that keeps thinking any minute the Colonel's Lincoln's gonna turn down the path to find our spot on the river. Colonel Henry will light his cigar, take off that beaver-skin hat and scratch his head while he tells me in Tennessee drawl to help Grandma with the food in the backseat. Their dinner leftovers will warm my hands through the foil Grandma wrapped around the plates and I'll feel that hot air from inside the car, just before it slips out into the dark morning frost and my face will remember what it felt like to not be outside, to not be here.

The only headlights we see for now are headed out to Mackinac Trail.

The night's catch steams in silver piles from buckets and trash bags in the bed of Dad's truck. A few smelt flop around in small empty spaces in the back. Some are just there, frozen to the wood on the bed. I love smelt dipping, but I hate that fish stink, and smelt, in these numbers, can do some real damage to your nostrils. It's that cold, muddy fish smell that grocery store fish can't match. The way they're piled up there, I'm not sure how we're gonna get back home, all six of us, without somebody sitting on a pile of fish. We really killed 'em tonight. There'll be smelt frying for weeks.

There's no good reason for me to go back down to the river, but I've got an urge to get down there one more time and feel the little scaly darts pull the net downcurrent. Dad and Tony found a campfire ring. They're smoking by the fire, roasting a couple smelt. Dad moves the stick to different spots in the pit to keep the little silver fish from burning. All three younger boys are sleeping in the cab of the truck, the windows fogged from their snoring. They all got mud on their jackets and pants. Ryan and Tommy got their sweatshirt hoods and gloves on. Johnny's wearing Dad's camouflage Budweiser cap with the brim loose over his eyes and nose. The cab smells like smelt, sweat and wet sand when I open up the truck for another trash bag.

"You going back down?" Dad asks me.

"We got enough damn smelt already, dude." Tony puffs and chokes a little on his joint. "It's not all about the fish."

"No, but the fishing makes it better," my old man says. "Come sit down, Buck. You're old enough to hear this."

I want to go back to the river. See the smelt caught in the steel mesh and feel the cold numb of the steel handle through my brown jersey gloves. The icy water of the Carp feels safer, warmer than Tony and Dad's cold faces over the fire pit. Dad points for me to stay put, so I take my seat on a half-slab of birch that'll feed the fire before dawn.

"Your Grampa was a good man," says Tony. "Gave me work and a place to stay when we got back from the war. I'd do anything for him."

"Can't do anything for him now, Uncle Tony," I say, feeling my chest ice up. "He's gone. Nobody gonna bring him back."

"He ain't coming back, but we sure's hell gonna do something about it," Dad says. "That's my old man. You listen to me and listen good, boy—I don't want you telling no one about this, not your mother, nobody. You got me?" His hazel eyes burn through my frosted soul. All I can do is nod and look down at the roots that stick out through the last few patches of ice.

Last year, out here at the Carp, the Colonel got into it good with Uncle Ray about church and God. Uncle Ray was talking about how Colonel Henry and Grandma Clio should just get married already, instead of living in sin. When Ray brought it up, made me sick to my gut. I never wanted to think about Grandma and Henry rolling around wrinkled and naked. Why would old people even want sex—leave the fucking to the young. Ray must've been thinking a lot about it though. Brought it up a few times before the Colonel told him to shut his "got-damned mouth."

Colonel Henry always says, "Ain't no bigger hypocrites than you'll find in church on Sunday, boy. Biggest sinners of 'em all." He gave old Ray an earful, and Ray mostly stood there shaking his head. Everybody knows Grandma Clio is the boss, but she let Henry go on, shooting Ray bad looks. Never seen Colonel Henry get so many words out without Grandma stopping him, but she was pissed off at Ray. Let old Henry lay into him. Seemed like every other word was a curse, but the Colonel cranks it up when he gets riled. Ray said something about blasphemy and the Colonel told him why should he care about a god who let him sit there and watch three of his brothers die in a coal mine.

"What kind of deity kills children and ruins the life of a nine-year-old-boy?" he asked Ray. Henry and five of his brothers fell in the shaft but only three made it out. "What the hell kind a faith a boy have in a god that cruel?" Henry told us how he never went to church after that. All this is probably the reason Ray didn't come out this year. Don't know why the Colonel and Grandma Clio didn't come though. They patch fights over a bottle of Scotch—never take anything too personal. Wherever they are, it's got to be warmer than here.

I wish I could go back and erase everything Tony and Dad told me about their revenge plan. I wish I was one of the younger boys, sleeping in the cab of the truck, even with all the stink. Lester Cronin's got it coming, but I never wanted to be drug into killing, even if it's for Grandpa. Makes sense now why Tony's keeping such a close eye on Lester. No surprise he's the one who's gonna take him down.

I'm sure it's personal too—not just about Grandpa. Tony's still sore over the Walleye contest. They say old Cronin cheated—caught fish after the deadline. Nobody could prove anything, the contest being on the honor system and all, but everybody knows Lester Cronin caught almost a pound after the deadline was over—stole second place and Tony's hundred-fifty dollar prize. Before Lacey left, that was all Tony would talk about when he got pissed-off drunk.

Tony got real fumed last week when Mom told him what happened with Lester's mother. Rumor is Lester killed her off with D-Con. Needed the inheritance money so he could keep his hardware store open. Rat poisoned her every day till she croaked. Nobody in town can prove that either, but everybody knows the truth.

I zip down my fly and piss by Dad's front truck tire. Try to get my jeans all the way back up while I walk past the fogged windows of the old Ford, north of the fire, but the zipper jams and pinches my pointing finger. When I get the zipper up, I suck the blood from my finger and grab that smelt net one more time. Walk the path down the hill to the river. Don't even look back up the ridge when somebody tries to start the truck. Could be that Tony and Dad had enough and are packing up, but it might be they're trying to keep the boys warm in the cab or to keep the battery from draining in the cold. The radio was on all night and half the morning so it needs a good charge.

The dim sunlight fights its way up from behind the birch and maples and paints a pink-red sky. Hard sand from the bank falls in chunks when I step in the wrong places. I feel drunk but I didn't touch any alcohol this time—not even a sniff of Dad or Tony's beer. The truck motor still won't start. It sounds like a hacksaw in rookie hands. After a few tries, somebody finally gets the engine to turn over. The eight track is blasting up on the ridge behind me. Sounds like Styx again. About three feet down, a big chunk of hard sand crumbles off the side. I try to grab the branches of the pine that grows crooked, almost sideways over the water, but it only keeps me up for a few more seconds. The tip of the tree bounces back like a slingshot, slapping me in the face.

The current pushes me away from the hill-top campsite where Dad's truck is parked. I don't yell, not even with the shock of the cold water. It's not that deep and I'm sure somebody heard the splash. I can't see anybody, just the cold red sunrise and the roots and trees that stick out the steep bank of the Carp. I try to pull myself out but my clothes are too heavy. The hip waders fill fast with river and it's all I can do to breathe, to keep my head above the dark water. The river thrashes me to a branch sticking out the right side bank hill. I grab the twisted cedar with frost-numb fingers. I think of Cody LeVassuer's cold, white and blue carcass. I'm stronger than him. I won't die in this river. The cold's loosening my grip, though, and the wet's prying my fingers from the branch. I hold on a good couple of minutes, then I give in and go where the river wants to take me. I fight with all the fight left in me to get back to the bank, but the water's too heavy. I paddle my arms and kick my legs, with nothing left but my adrenaline. My body gives out so I rest a few seconds and try to do it again, but all the muscle in my arms and legs is gone. I'm scared when my head goes under but it feels kind of peaceful, in a way, cause I'm so tired.

Last summer, a couple months after Henry and Ray's big fight, Dad and old Henry got into some deep bullshitting when we were cooking burgers and brats out at the dunes. Henry says he's mostly an atheist but he could be wrong. There could be a God—nobody knows for sure. Guess that's the best anybody's got to go with. Doesn't calm me much, not knowing what's next, but the river's taking me down, taking me with her, and nothing I do can change that. My head gives way to the Carp's brown current.

After the other boys fell asleep, Tony finished his Army story. He said that him and Dad took turns carrying the baby girl, but Dad carried it more than Tony.

"Don't know how he did it," Tony said, "humping the sixty and all. My fat ass had a hard enough time without the baby, but I tried to pull my weight."

He said that the baby was good luck. Not a shot was fired the three days they carried that baby. They fed her water and coffee through a green nipple they rigged up out of rain gear.

"You would've thought it was a real tit the way that baby would suck on that thing," Tony said. "We left it with a little girl the first village we come across. Humped a good thirty miles that day and then the shit got real hot. Took three, no, four KIA, in our platoon alone in a roadside ambush that day. Can you believe that, Buck?" He told me. "A baby, right there, in the middle of the fucking jungle."

A single hand rips me out of the river with a pull like a steel crane. That kind of force, it's got to be Uncle Tony. All I feel is the hand and the suction of the river, until the iced air stings through my soaked clothes and works its way to my head. I feel punching on my chest, steady and strong till I chunk out water. Everything feels hard and real again. Then I see the face with the hands. It's Dad, not Tony.

"Gonna be a cold ride home," he says. "Told you keep your head up. Got to keep your goddamn head up, boy."

1994

I used to get a letter a week from Katherine Beckett. That ended a few months back. Sergeant Sollivan, a drill sergeant I had back at basic, told us that nothing ever changes back home and we should never worry about home—he'd been in for twenty-six years and everything was always the same as when he left it. He couldn't be more wrong. Katherine's married now and she was a big part of the reason why I'm here, trying to better myself. Nothing changes is bullshit. Everything changes fast. A few months back, Johnny told me that one of my best friends, Ronnie LeVasseur, died in a head on collision with a tractor trailer. Alcohol was a factor. Ronnie fell asleep at the wheel they said. Some people think it was suicide but nobody can prove it—just gossip around town. Sometimes I wonder if I would have been around, there's that chance I would've run into Ronnie, had a couple beers and talked about all the good times. He might not have been driving eighty miles an hour down M-134 in the wrong lane.

Ronnie saved my life when I was sixteen. We were all partying out at the old rock quarry lake on Jamison Road, just off Mackinac Trail. Wasn't even that drunk, but I landed wrong diving in, started to suck in water. It was pitch dark so I panicked. Couldn't tell where I was. Went under a couple of times, just like the time I almost drown in the Carp River when I was a kid. Don't know how Ronnie knew I was drowning but the next thing I knew, he was there pulling me up. My weight brought him under a few times but he never let go—had his arms locked around my chest and told me to calm down or we'd both be dead. That we'd both be going under. When I thanked him later on for saving my life, he just told that he wasn't afraid to die. Said he could see his brother in the afterlife. I'll never get to repay Ronnie now. Things change. Couple new businesses popped up while I was gone too, a couple closed down. Shit sure as hell will change when I get back.

Couldn't sleep last night so I pulled duty until 4:00 AM, let the other guys sleep a while. Captain Stubbs ordered me to rest so I got into my sleeping bag and tried to calm. Almost fell asleep but I heard Wiggins and Robinson with pickaxe and shovel, going at it, digging a new latrine at first daylight. I'd start to nod off and Wiggins would run his mouth. Even Robinson's voice was more irritating than usual. They kept laughing about something. Then I had a sort of daydream that I was back in high school and we were camping out on Marquette Island. A bunch of us were sitting around the fire and talking about music. My high school friends were there, like Jay and Ronnie, but so were Robinson, Van Dorn and Wiggins. Wiggins started talking about all the things he was going to do to Katherine Beckett and I told him to shut up or I'd kick his ass. Then everybody was laughing at me when Stubb woke me up. Told me to get some grub and get back at it—that two hours was enough sleep. Bet I didn't get more than five minutes of sleep. I ate a turkey pack from an MRE and then I was up digging a new position. Stubb thought it was best to dig in around the perimeter, just in case somebody came looking for the Bosnian.

Now it's noon and we're back at the cardboard Spades table. My hands shake the whole time. Didn't notice anything when I was digging, but my whole body's shivering now.

"Damn, hero, what's wrong with them hands?" Robinson asks.

"Good thing he didn't shake like that with that sniper rifle," Wiggins says. He imitates an epileptic seizure and Robinson laughs and calls him stupid. Van Dorn looks at me and shakes his head.

It's hard to focus on the game—keep thinking of back home. I'm close to getting shipped back, but Stubb says I might get stop-lossed if the DOD wants to. Every minute I spend here is fucking with my brain. I feel a dizzy sort of adrenaline rush come on, drop my cards, face-up, even though we're in the middle of the game and walk to the steel concertina wire post were my gear hangs. I'm sweating and I feel my whole body shaking, not just my hands.

"You done fucked up the game, Willie," Wiggins yells out at me.

"I'm done, Wig" I say. "Get somebody else to play."

"Let's take a break, boys," Van Dorn says. "Give this boy some time to collect himself."

"All my socks smell like shit," I say. "Gonna go down to the river and scrub some clothes."

"Ain't no more soap," Robinson says.

"Got a bar from back home. I might to join you," says Van Dorn. He's hardly said a word to anybody since we all met up here and I can tell he's got something to tell me, so I nod my head and thank him for sharing his soap.

Halfway down the hill, Van Dorn pulls a clear plastic bottle out his green laundry sack.

"Got me some hooch," he says. "Pap sent it from back home. Hid it with the rock candy and kippered jerky."

He hands me the bottle and I get the first pull.

"Don't say nothing to these other boys. They don't deserve Pap's whiskey."

I just nod again. Van Dorn takes a drink and hands the bottle back to me.

"Hell of a shot you made. Everybody else here is all talk, but you're the kind of guy can get it done."

"No I'm not," I tell him. "Think I closed my eyes before I squeezed it out. Just want to do my time and get home."

"Amen to that, brother," he says. "Have another shot. Gonna write Pap. Tell him to mail you a bottle too."

There was a time I almost forgot about Lester Cronin, all caught up in baseball, the parties, the girls. Then one day Chad Cronin got drunk at a party and told me he could take me out just like his grandpa took out Grandpa Eddie. I just froze up like a pussy and didn't do anything cause I was so shocked he'd just admit to it in front of everybody. After Uncle Jack missed the shot on Lester Cronin, everybody thought it was best to wait a long while before we tried to get revenge again. I got a baseball scholarship and tried to focus on college but I flunked out the first semester cause I couldn't think about anything but Grandpa. Was only a half-assed college player too, even though I was all-state baseball in high school. That really got me to drinking harder.

One game in high school, almost hit for the cycle. Had a homerun, triple and a couple singles. Went four for five but it should've been five for five. Some lucky third baseman was cheating over to the middle and a hard liner one-hopped into his glove. Would've been extra bases for sure. I was all riled, shaking and pissed off. Would've loved to have just one game like that in college, but I really stunk it up. Never realized how good I had it in college, though. Worst day there was better than the best day here. Still, these guys here, with all their problems, are like family. Can't say that about any of the guys on the baseball team or in the dorms. If I got to be stuck in some shithole halfway around the world, at least I'm in good company.

Major Hansen came back to let us know he called higher up. Let us know the Australians are sending in a team to investigate the Bosnian on the hill. "Took a while cause everything here is such a clusterfuck," he says. Then he congratulates me on the shot.

"Metzger's a short-timer," says Stubb. "We're sending him back to the civilian world with a long-range kill. What better gift could a CO give his soldier?"

"Sure you don't want to re-enlist?" Perry asks me.

"Hell no. This boy's officer material," says Hansen. "Ought to send you off to OCS."

I have no intention of becoming an officer or re-enlisting, but I tell them all that I'll think about my options. I've only got one choice, the way I see it—time to get back to unfinished business in the civilian world. Time to get my revenge on Lester Cronin.

In the letter my brother Johnny sent me, he told me that the guy Katherine Beckett was getting married to was some accountant from Ann Arbor. Thought I would want to know. I went on a few dates with Katherine my senior year of high school. Everything was going great until one day we were out in Hessel Bay in her parents' new boat. It was a double cabin cruiser and Katherine's dad was really proud of it. They always had money but Katherine's grandma died and left him a whole shitload more. Then Mr. Beckett started getting snottier than ever. He took me aside that day and told me that I shouldn't get so serious with Katherine. She should marry an attorney or a doctor. I told him that I could go to law school or medical school and he told me it wasn't the same—I'd be starting with nothing. A girl like Katherine deserved a doctor with a trust fund, a "lineage," like he said. I always thought I could get ahead faster in life if I found a way to pay for college. I thought maybe Katherine would wait for me. That's another reason I joined the Army. Now I know how stupid I was. These guys, with their panty boxes and threats for divorce with day after day make-up sex in non-deployment and all the perversions, what they got is real, not some bullshit dream like I had with Katherine.

It's almost sundown. I stand on the edge of the hill behind the old stone building and stare out at the hill where I took down the Bosnian. A Zippo clicks open behind me. Sergeant Perry lights a Pall Mall and offers me one. I don't want it but I take it cause it helps calm the shaking.

"Didn't hear me come up behind you, did you? Better get over it and get your head out your ass. Somebody's gonna come looking for that sniper, so you better be ready. Don't know who or how many, but they're coming, and we're in a big clusterfuck here, undermanned, under-experienced. I need you on your game, Sarge."

"I'll get it together, First Sergeant. Just need some rest."

"Why don't you get back to the card table with the boys. Get your mind off things."

"Kind of tired of playing Spades. I'd kill for a game of Euchre."

"What the fuck is that? Never heard of Euchre. Why don't y'all play a good old-fashioned game of Poker. I'd get in on that."

"You trust those boys with money on the line?"

"Son, everybody cheats at Poker. Just got to learn to out cheat the cheaters. Boy, you look like shit."

"I feel worse."

"Things could always be worse. In the Gulf War, was in a mechanized unit. We were in the south, patrolling the border with Kuwait, and they sent us out to take out some Iraqi regulars. On the way there, this dumb-fuck private—Skinner was his name—was riding in the back of my Bradley with the barrel of his SAW pointed up. I'd been back there, would've told him to keep the barrel down cause he could've unloaded on everybody. I was up in the turret, though, crew commander. Just breaking in a new driver—that boy was having a hell of a time getting used to driving like that, looking through the periscopes. Hit a ditch and Skinner's SAW was locked and loaded. He was ready to come out the back shooting. Blew his own damn head off."

Perry looks like he's gonna cry, then he starts to laugh until he coughs and almost chokes.

"With all due respect, Top, what's so damn funny?"

"Least we're not Skinner."

1984

Reynosa's not a Clint Eastwood border town with sombreros, vaqueros and six shooters. It's not cigars, tequila and bandoleers or leather-saddled horses with shotgun holsters and fire horns. It's city-dirty, traffic and sweat. Grandpa's truck's in a dirt lot in Hidalgo, Texas, right across the bridge. Jack drives it now, since Grandpa disappeared. Dad was afraid we'd get lost driving in Mexico, so Jack just parked it over there.

The three of us walk up to Mexican customs and the moustached man in green waves us through. A short woman in a dark blue jumpsuit scrubs the sidewalk with a pushbroom and soap water. She pours green liquid from a bottle that says "Fabuloso" over a black patch on the cement. It smells like flowers, dust and Lysol all around. There's a long row of taxis on the other side of the Mexican customs building where the traffic from the bridge meets the narrow streets. Dad and Uncle Jack just ignore the drivers. They all look me in the eyes and I tell them "No gracias" every time one of them says, "Taxi." They all look as desperate as old man Edgar begging for whiskey outside George White's Amoco station back in Cedarville. One taxi driver wipes his forehead with his silk purple shirt sleeve and the others point to their cabs. Their smiles only last till we walk by.

A dust-faced boy, can't be older than seven, tries to sell us cigarettes and gum and follows us all the way to a black, cast-iron bench in the plaza. Jack stomps his foot at him but he doesn't go away until Dad buys a pack of Marlboros, fifty cents.

Jack wipes his forehead with a red and black hankie. His face looks like a riping tomato and sweat comes down like a creek on his chin. We all put on fresh t-shirts in the morning, but now they're wet as car wash rags.

Dad lights up a smoke.

"The truck okay there cross the river?" He holds the box of Marlboros out to me and Uncle Jack. Jack shakes his head no, but I light one up. This is only the second time Dad ever let me smoke.

"Nobody wants that piece of shit Dodge, Gene," says Jack. "How many times it break down on the way here?"

"Guy at the gas pumps in McAllen says the bus station just a couple blocks from here," Dad says.

"Should've asked him which direction," I tell him.

"Finish these smokes and we'll start walking that way," Dad says. "We'll run into somebody tell us which way to go. You just keep track of the money. Still got that stash in your pocket, Buck? Gonna need that when we get back."

I start to pull the wad out my right jean pocket. He gives me a not here look. Then he just nods and slaps me hard on the back. He flicks his Marlboro down and crushes it into the dusty concrete with his brown, steel-toed boot. The letter is wadded up in the back pocket of his blue Carharts. Uncle Tony wrote that note, leaving everything he owned to Dad. That was before he pulled the trigger and painted the kitchen wall with his blood and brain chunks. It was the old man and me found him there, sitting at the kitchen table with the note. First line was, "To my friends: sorry to cash out early. Everybody else can suck it!" The rest of the letter was kind of boring—a dead man's unfinished business.

Tony was supposed to help with the revenge but he couldn't keep his shit together. Left the rest of us to take care of it. Nobody blamed him though, with everything Lacey put him through. He was loyal as a son to Grandpa. When I heard young Chad Cronin bragging to the Adams boys about what old Lester did to Grandpa, Tony was the first one I told. He was ready for war. Just wasn't ready for Lacey—banging all those other guys and messing with his head when he found out about it.

A blonde girl in a red, silk shirt and black miniskirt waves at us from a side street. There's a row of dusty orange and brown cement houses and a corner store with a Carta Blanca sign on our left side, and a dirt mound wall on the other side of the road. Old

Volkswagen Beetles and beat up pick-ups with chipped, faded paint line both sides.

The girl waves again.

"Well look at that," says Dad.

"Hey, you guys. Come here to me, please," she yells to us. "Yes, you."

"She speaks good English. Maybe she can help us find the bus station," I say.

She's thin and curvy and Jack gives Dad a look and whistles. The closer we get to her, the happier she looks, but her face changes. Thought she was a woman in her twenties, but she's probably not much older than me. She's wearing too much makeup and her dye job is school bus blonde. She has the wide, brown, glossy eyes of an older woman. Her black, high-heel boots make her look taller than she really is, but she's still a couple inches shorter than me. She holds out her hand to Jack, palm down, like a princess in a movie. Her smile shrinks when Jack just shakes her hand. Can't say for sure if she's nervous or maybe a little shifty.

"I'm Ana," she says. "What is your names?"

"Gene." Dad holds out his hand. Ana rubs his arm.

"You have sexy muscles. And, you are a cute one," she tells me. "What are you sexy men looking for in Reynosa?"

Dad pulls out a Marlboro and lights up. "Bus Station. You know where we go to catch a bus to Acapulco?"

"Give me a cigarette and I tell you."

"Aren't you a little young to smoke," says Jack.

"Not too young to show you things," she says.

"I bet," says the old man. Ana lights up and points to the opposite direction of where we were walking.

"Go that way two streets and pass the plaza. Then you go right three or four streets. Then you cross and go left. The bus is straight of there."

"Is that the Rio Grande on the other side of that mound," I ask.

"It is the Rio Bravo," says Ana.

"Damned if it don't look like the Rio Grande," says Jack. "Couldn't be though, or we're walking the wrong way."

"In US, it called Rio Grande. In Mexico, it is Rio Bravo," she tells us.

"Sounds like a bullshit story to me," Dad says, kind of quiet. "Name's already in Mexican, why would they change it here."

It's got to be a hundred degrees, but Ana isn't sweating and it looks like she's been outside for a while. Her boots are dusty around the bottom from the street, but most of the leather is so shiny it almost hurts my eyes to look down. For the first time, I smell my own stink. It's like three-day underwear mixed with that old coin hand smell. Ana smells like tangerines. She snares us in with those bright eyes and her pink grizzly lips.

"I have a place," she says. "You could come inside."

"We got to get going," the old man says. "Gotta catch a bus."

"Maybe I'll catch you on the way back," says Uncle Jack.

I wave to her and smile and we walk toward the plaza.

"Hey sexy," she says, "can I have another cigarette?"

The old man looks down at the pack of Marlboros and starts to take one out. He puts it back and tosses the pack to Ana.

"Thank you, Mister Muscles," she tells him.

This is my first time in Mexico. First time out of the country, really, unless you count Canada. I've never seen a place like this before. There's hardly no trees and everything's dusty brown. The streets smell like old rust and sewer. I should pay more attention to Reynosa but Jack and Dad are walking fast and I got to keep up. I'm tired from the trip. Too tired to think. Too tired to take it all in without worrying about everything back home.

The people here—they see us. Some give us funny looks, some smile and the rest of them don't pay us any attention. The farther away from the bridge we get, people aren't so pushy. Hardly nobody asks for money now, but just about everybody's selling something: Rottweiler puppies, chrome car parts—all kinds of food: burgers, tacos, strange red and white meat spinning around on a metal rod. Too hot to think about food, though. The only place I know that's hotter than this is a sauna. Like the one out at the Browns' place. We'd all go ice fishing out there in McKay Bay. Tony, Jay and Dad would leave a few twelve-packs in the snow bank. Around dark, we'd fire up the sauna. Once it got nice and hot, we'd all pile in and see who could stand it the longest. After the older guys had a few beers, they'd run barefoot on the Lake Huron ice. Sometimes me and the younger boys did it too.

One time Tony drank so much he passed out in the sauna. He was in there a good twenty minutes before anybody noticed. Bet he felt this kind of hot tired. Hot like Reynosa. No green, no trees except for a palm or mesquite here and there. What would you do for firewood around here?

Ana gave good directions, so the bus stop was easy to find. We finally figured out they call it the "central." Inside, the bus station is a little cooler than outside, but not much. They got fans blowing and a place to sit down, so it beats walking around the street. Dad brings tacos and Cokes from a stand outside the bus station.

"You gotta try this, boys. This is some good shit," he tells us, salsa running down his upper lip and a piece of tortilla in his moustache.

"I'd eat the ass out of a puppy," says Uncle Jack.

"Cheap too," says the old man, "only paid five bucks for all this."

He's right— they are good. Best tacos I ever had. My favorite Mexican restaurant is a place in the Sault. The tacos are good there, just different than here. More cheese and harder tortillas. Place is called the Palace. Tony used to take us there. Every time he'd get drunk and tell us how the Mexican food was so much better in the Rio Grande Valley. Mr. Miller saw Tony with Lacey at the Palace two weeks before he shot himself. I heard Miller talking to Mr. Roth about it at school. He said Lacey gave Tony a lap dance right at the table when "Whole Lotta Love" came on the jukebox. She knocked the nachos off the table with her ass and the waitress told her to leave or she'd call the cops.

We could really use Tony about now. My Spanish isn't good enough to understand the ticket guy and nobody else here is helping. Tony always said he could get by with his Spanish, even though he didn't know as much as the rest of his family. Funny, the only family Tony ever really talked about was his little sister Lucy and his dad. His old man was career military. Saw some heavy action in WWII and Korea but was lucky through most of it. Not even a scratch on him till a Belgian hooker knifed him into a coma in Amsterdam. He went on special leave when he found out Tony and Lucy's mom was fucking around on him with a young captain. Never made it back to base. Died from stab wound infections. Tony never wanted anything to do with his mom after that, and he didn't say much more about family. Except for Lucy. Always said he missed her. Tony's land is on the Texas side of the river, in Mission. After we leave Jack at the bus stop, we're going to see about it and meet Lucy. Tell her the bad news.

A slick-haired guy in a white-collared shirt and a black vest walks behind the ticket counter and says something to the guy who can't understand me. He nods and smiles at us.

"To where you go, gentlemen?" he asks.

"A beach somewhere would be nice," says Jack. "How about Acapulco?"

"How long a trip is that?" Dad asks.

"Maybe one day and a half," says the man, "if you get connections on time. We have no direct bus. You go for vacation, yes. I print for you the tickets?"

"Give us a minute," says Jack. "We need to talk about this."

The man smiles and says something in Spanish to the other man about a girl named Marisol.

"Let's get a beer," says Dad. "We need to work this out with clear heads."

There's a bar back home they call the Skunk House. The real name is Little Ricky's—they just call it Skunk House cause it's painted black and white and smells like skunk. Outsiders call it a dive, but it's not. It's where the locals drink their beers. Been there a few times with Mom to pick up Tony and Dad when they're too drunk to get the keys in the ignition. Mom sends me in to get them cause she don't want anybody to see her in there. Not sure what she's worried about—you can barely see your hand three feet in front of your face through the smoke. Every kind of rotgut whiskey, vodka and tequila you can imagine sits on the cedar board behind the bar. On tap, they got the cheapest beer in town. That's why Dad and Tony called it home.

It's hard to walk in the Skunk House. Your shoes stick to the floor the minute you step in. Some of the scariest women I've ever seen would stare at me like I was a piece of venison. There's almost always some kind of fight or yelling going on in that place. The cantina across from the bus station makes the Skunk House look fancy.

"Dos cervezas por favor," says Dad. "And a Coke for the kid."

"Y una Coca Cola, verdad," says the man at the bar.

We take our bottles to a tall table with no chairs.

"I can't do this Gene," Uncle Jack says. "It's not as easy as in the movies. Nobody speaks English here. And what do I do for work? All's I got is four hundred dollars."

"Can't go back home," Dad says. "Can't risk it with the law. You sure Cronin saw your face."

"I think so. Not sure. Hell, I was so nervous—almost pissed my pants. Maybe he didn't see nothing."

Dad puts his arm around Jack's shoulder. "You had the tough part—did your best."

"No Gene. I fucked it up. I closed my eyes when I went for the shot. I tried to think of a fourteen point buck like you said. Couldn't get over he was a man."

"Ain't much of a man," I say. "If it would've been me, I would've put it right between his fucking eyes after what he did to Gramps."

"Shut your mouth, boy" Dad tells me. "You don't know what you'd do till you do it. Not Jack's fault. Tony was supposed to take the shot."

"Why didn't you take it?" I ask him. "You got more experience."

"Jack's a better shot than me with the bow and arrow. He done better than I would've."

The bartender drops two more bottles on the table even though nobody ordered them. Dad pays and points to a pack of smokes. The girl with pink lipstick tosses the pack over from behind the bar. Dad walks to the window and lights one up. He stares out like someone's looking back at him, but nobody's there. Jack rubs his scalp with the palms of his hands. The bald spot on top of his blonde hair is sunset red. It's quiet in the bar and the crowd to the busses is slowed.

"Better watch that mouth, you little cocksucker," Uncle Jack tells me.

Jack should've been a senior in high school this September. In about two months, he would've started football practice. He was an all-conference linebacker and right guard last year. He might've married Holly Miller after graduation. Had three kids. Probably would've worked at the docks and played poker every Saturday at Ernie Roth's. Now he's homeless. Dad says maybe Jack could live in Uncle Tony's trailer in Mission until he works everything out. Maybe Lucy could line up a job for him where she works: a place where they make packaged food for the Army, MREs. Tony always told Dad if times got tough they could work there or in the oilfields out by McCook. Only problem's getting back over the border now without getting caught.

I wonder if Grandpa had any idea when he crossed the bridge into Canada that Cronin was out to get him. It's no secret Grandpa and old Lester Cronin weren't best of friends when they headed off to Ontario for their moose hunting trip. They used to be real close. Went to Canada together every year since Grandpa moved up from Detroit in the 50's. Dad, Uncle Ray, Johnny, Grandma and me were all there when Grandpa and Lester packed up the trailer, just like every other year. They went in Lester's truck but only Lester came back three weeks later. He said he got in a fight with Gramps and left him at the bus station in Wawa. He acted surprised around Grandma when he came back. Said Grandpa should've been back a week early. Everyone who knows Grandpa knows that isn't true. He'd be out there every day trying to get his moose. Shane Grady told me that he heard Chad Cronin bragging about how Lester shot Grandpa in the back with his 30-06. Said he didn't die right away so Lester beat him with a wooden maul handle and buried him under a Lake Superior beach.

Dad thinks Lester owed Gramps some money and didn't want to pay up. Mom heard gossip that Grandpa had a thing with Agnes Cronin. All we know for sure is that there's no body and it's a safe bet nobody's ever going to find one. If it would've been a fair fight, Lester would've never left Canada.

By the time Dad and Jack finish up their beers, the sun is lower, moving toward the upstream side of the river. The bartender points us back in the direction of the bridge, right where Dad said it would be. Our shirts are sweat-stained, but not as wet as before. Smoke-white clouds puff out everywhere in the baby-blue sky over the Rio Grande. It seems deeper than the dark sky back home.

Jack's got a good buzz, but Dad keeps a straight face for all that beer they drank. At the cantina, he gave me a half a bottle of Dos Equis and said, "That's enough for you. Don't tell your mother about that cigarette I let you smoke either."

"This place ain't so bad," Jack says. "People seem real nice. Might stay here if I could understand all that Mexican talk."

"It's called Spanish," I tell him, but they don't say anything.

We walk by city blocks, with red, white and brown-painted brick and adobe houses. Most have black or white steel bars in the windows and chain-locked gates in front. There's a bank, a taco stand and a dark, wrinkled lady selling some kind of ice cream from a pushcart.

"Wonder how they keep it cold?" Jack asks.

There's a girl across the street with long blonde hair and a short black skirt.

"Wonder if that's Ana," Dad says.

There's something about that Ana that reminds me of Anna James back home, except this Ana's the Mexican version. It's in their faces, the shape, the look, the blonde color of their hair. Anna James is in Europe by now. She cried in front of everybody at one of our baseball games. I was in the on-deck circle and I heard her scream from the bleachers behind home plate. She threw a tantrum cause she didn't get to Rome last year. Even after Mr. James told her he'd take the family to Italy this summer, she still sniffled and pouted through the rest of our game. I wonder what the Mexican Ana would think about Rome. I'm sure I'll never see it.

The blonde girl flirts with a man in a blue uniform. Maybe a cop. When we get closer we see that she's older than Ana by at least twenty years. Her face is wrinkled under the white-powder make-up and her eyes cold, narrow and brown.

"Wonder how long she's been at it?" Jack asks.

"Long enough to catch some gonorrhea," Dad says.

"Is there a cure for that?" I ask him.

"There's a cure for pretty much everything, Son. Except death. You probably take care of gonorrhea with some penicillin."

The woman gets into a small Toyota truck with the man in the uniform. We watch him light her cigarette before they drive away and turn left by the river wall. The bridge is straight to our right.

"Texas," says Jack.

We stop and look up at the light blue sky one more time, then walk. On the trip down, we saw a young red-haired girl hitching a ride on an eighteen-wheeler at a truck stop. We heard her say she was from Boston. Dad just shook his head and said, "Wonder how she ended-up in Tennessee. So far from home. So far from her family and her roots."

Last November, Uncle Tony, me and Jack were playing Euchre. Tony said his roots were deep in the Rio Grande Valley. After Jack and Tony left, I asked Dad about our roots.

"Deep as the cedars. Stronger than the jackpine. We've got roots, boy."

Ana's Rio Bravo curls in from the west, slow and muddy toward the bridge. Jack takes another deep breath. The brown waters of the Tahquamenon and the Carp are different than the brown I see in the river under the guardrail.

We walk to the halfway point of the bridge. There's a copper plaque that marks the U.S. and Mexican sides of the border. Dad turns to say something to Jack but he's not there. He's standing a hundred yards back, staring at us, froze up, from just past the toll gate.

1995

I've got a bad case of the spleen. That's some old fashion talk Colonel Henry uses—says it means you're so pissed off there's hardly a cure but to let loose—go all out on somebody or something. I'm trying to keep my shit together though cause Dad says I can stay at home, long as I do my part and act like family—don't go apeshit. Whiskey's always good to take the edge off, so I stop by the only gas station left in town that has a liquor license, Torrio's. Normally I'd buy a fifth but I pick-up a half gallon of Kessler's, to share with the family. If I keep it together this time, I get a second chance—warm bed, shower, food—time to save up for college. No more living in my car. Jobs are hard to come by these days, but I'm gonna look for something, even if it's part-time, first thing next week. On the way out the gas station, I grab the twenty pound bag of ice I paid for with the whiskey. There's a bright purple Camaro parked next to my Buick. Chad Cronin steps out, slicked back brown hair, thin-framed sunglasses and a brown leather coat. His clothes look expensive, but they're at least a size too big for his scrawny frame.

"Hey," I tell him, but his shoes squeak as he walks right past. "Like you don't fucking see me, Cronin," I say.

He turns back for a second and stares at me without a word, then turns to pull the glass door open.

"Well fuck you," I say.

He turns his head to me again and smiles. I think I hear him say something like, "Fuck your grandpa," but I'm not sure. Ever since Grandpa Eddie disappeared, he's always looked at me the same way, with that smirk.

I sit in the Buick with my door open, twist off the half gallon's cap. I might normally just drink straight from the bottle but I've got a plastic cup and a bag of ice, so I pour a few shots on the rocks and wait for Chad. After four or five good swigs, my head warms and my arms vibrate from the shoulders. I might just follow Chad, see if he stops somewhere with nobody else around. I pour more Kessler's into the cup but Chad's still inside, taking his time. I'm thinking what I'm gonna say when I hear a pounding on the passenger side window. It's Tommy. Dad's in the truck.

"Get in," he says. "Bring the hooch, that half gallon you got. We're gonna see the Colonel. Grandma called—said he's asking for us."

I roll up the window and lock the Buick doors. Chad walks out when Dad turns right toward the blinker light. Chad stares for a second at the Buick and gets into the Camaro. He follows Dad's pick-up until the school, then he turns south on Beach Street.

"Pass me the whiskey," Dad says. "Gonna need it."

Grandma Clio and Henry have a place out on Drummond Island, on the northwest side where the St. Mary's feeds into Lake Huron. It's not a big house—just a small cottage with two bedrooms and a closet-sized shower in the laundry room. There's a big yard, though, evergreens, birch and a large chunk of waterfront with a cedar dock that stretches out as far as the rich folks' piers—it's big enough to keep a yacht in deep water, but the only thing tied to the cedar posts is Henry's old fishing boat, 40 horse Evinrude, oars and a stack of red life vests nobody's ever used. Grandma and Henry take good care of the cottage—there's a fresh coat of dark green paint on the exterior and garage. The sun is bright over the water and plants are sprouting all around the yard through the brown grass, but a cool wind blows through every few minutes and reminds us that summer isn't that close yet. Grandma meets us at the door with a yellow flyswatter in her right hand. It's the first time since I've known Henry that he's not at the door when we got there. It's the first since I can remember that their little black dog, Lethe, isn't at the door either. Mom says they put that old girl down seven months ago. She was a mutt puppy they found on the side of the road and she ended-up living another seventeen years. Grandma smiles, pats me on the back with her left hand and pulls me toward her tiny body for a kiss on the cheek. She does the same to my brother Tommy, then she gets serious and looks toward the woodshed.

"It's been a while since you seen Henry, Buck," Grandma says. "He's not the same man he was a couple years ago." She swats at a mosquito until the buzzing stops.

"How is the old man?" Dad asks.

"Let's get a beer," she says.

Henry's in the living room, hunched over in his recliner, about a hundred pounds lighter than the last time I saw him. Loose skin hangs between his chin and neck and his eyes are sunk deeper into his head. His long thin legs are resting, bent straight and proper, but his upper body is slouched in the chair. His skin's a yellow-tanned color and he's wearing the same buckskin vest he always wears to fish or duck hunt, but he's got on flannel pajama bottoms for pants. Henry loves the rivers and lakes—always said it was that and Grandma kept him here all these years. Much as he loved Tennessee, this was his home too. Still, Henry always talked a lot about things he missed from the south. Before his father died, he said the whole family would travel around from Tennessee to Georgia to Kentucky and Mississippi and back—all over the place.

One time I took a trip from Fort Benning to Haynes Lake, Mississippi with one of my platoon buddies, Hal Killegrew. Drove all around through the deep south. After I got out, he came up to the U.P. to visit. It was in early October. Most people who come to Les Cheneaux do it in warmer weather. It's mostly a summer tourist area. Outsiders usually go on about how beautiful the eastern U.P. is—Huron's blue and that evergreen smell— but they're only there for the one season and don't get the whole picture. Hal got it from the first day there. He told me, "Man, northern Michigan is a lot like Stone County but it's colder and the lakes are bigger. Even got a road called Dixie Highway." On our drive out to Tahquamenon, he told me he wanted to come back to see the winter and summer, but he's been busy working for the family business, laying brick, and I don't feel much like talking to anybody lately either, so we're out of touch.

When I left for the Army, Henry was tight with the family. Now some of the family don't even talk to Henry anymore since he buddied up to Lester Cronin like a traitor. When the plan to kill

Lester Cronin fell through, everybody involved backed off from messing with Lester so nobody would be suspect. Then they all cooled off and sort of forgot about it. Uncle Ray told me that Henry even got to the point where he would drink shots with Lester at the West Entrance bar in Hessel. This didn't sit well with the family at first, but everybody got over it. They invited Henry to fewer Metzger family get-togethers until everybody saw less and less of him and Grandma, even though Henry and Grandma used to be real close to Dad's side of the family.

"What the hell do y'all want," Henry says. "Ain't nobody said hardly a word to me in a year. What you want now?"

"Been busy, Henry," says Dad. "Construction work's been steady. Putting up a new hotel in town and renovation work out at LaSalle Island."

"Y'all are my kin," says Henry. "Love you more than my blood kin and you leave me rot like some kind of leper. Try to make some damned excuse."

"No excuses here," I tell him. "Been discharged a while but I heard about you and Cronin. Didn't feel much like talking to you. Sitting at the bar with Lester all the time I was in the Army? You told me we were going after him when I got out. Then you're drinking whiskey with the devil himself."

"Oh, I got to know Lester Cronin and he weren't no devil. I followed through with the plan alright, Boy."

"What plan?" Tommy asks.

"Cronin had a heart attack," I tell him. "Some plan—sit around and wait for him to die."

"Easy, Son," says Dad. "Henry's not feeling well. Don't want to get him all worked up. What's this plan Henry?"

"It was between me and the boy, Gene. Promised Buck I'd help him take down Cronin years back when y'all Metzgers cluster fucked the first plan. Lester didn't die from a heart attack. Died like a gotdamn rat—the way he deserved."

"How you figure," Dad says. "Paper said Cronin died of natural causes."

"He's just senile—the Colonel wouldn't hurt his drinking buddy," I say.

Henry grabs my arm, with more strength than he should have,

and then his hand slides down the sleeve of my green sweatshirt and stares deep in my eyes till I keep my focus on his face.

"I drank Scotch. Lester was drinking Scotch and D-Con," Henry says. "My treat. Kept it in a Ziploc bag and I'd slip him a few grains every chance I got. It was easy in the dark, everybody drunk. Nobody pays attention to old men at the bar."

Tommy, Dad and I all stare at each other.

"Why you never tell anyone this, Henry. Hell, you could've made things better the last couple years."

"Nobody asked. Besides, you Metzgers would have fucked it all up again. You're good folk, but it's all or nothing with y'all, no second or third gear. Don't have a damned lick of patience, any one of you. Hot-tempered sons of bitches."

"I thought you and me planned this together," I tell him.

"You were the back-up plan," says Henry. "If the poison didn't get Lester, you would've. Always hoped it wouldn't get that far and I'm glad it didn't. Will y'all give me a minute alone with Buck?"

Dad and Tommy walk out to the kitchen with Grandma and the nurse. Grandma tells them she'll fry up some bacon and eggs. Toast some rye bread. Then Dad and Grandma whisper something with the nurse I can't hear.

"Look at me, Boy," Henry says. "Just what I thought. You got you a kill or two. Don't lie to me—it's just a fact. I can read your eyes. Didn't I teach you better than that, all those years of poker. Gave away your hand, Son." He laughs until he coughs and chucks out phlegm.

"All those years of you cheating—dealing from the bottom of the deck," I say. "That what you taught me?"

Henry coughs again and cuffs me across the cheek with his right hand with all the force he's got left. It stings.

"I do what I gotta and I always did what I had to. Always tried to protect you. Protect all you Metzgers. What you riled up about? No blood on your hands this way. None on your daddy's."

"I got blood, just not the blood I was looking for. Revenge on Cronin was part of the reason I enlisted—you know that. You told me to be patient and we'd get Cronin together."

"This deal with Cronin goes back before your grandpa, you see. Someday you'll thank me you didn't have to pull that trigger.

It's one thing to kill on the battlefield, another to do it domestic. Most of life is a poker game, son. Not a crap shoot."

Henry stares at his favorite book on the lamp table—first English edition of a book called *Thus Spoke Zarathustra*—read a lot of books in the last few years, but never that one, even though Henry always swore by it. He points to it.

"Pick it up," he tells me. "Take care of this for me. Want you to promise you'll read it."

"I can't keep this," I say, but he presses it into my hands. "I'll read it and give it back." He coughs and shakes his head no, then he holds out his arms to pull me in closer and kisses the top of my head, something he never even did when I was a kid.

"You're a good boy," he tells me. "Gonna do great things. I always took care of you, right?"

I nod yes to him.

"Take care of that book for me," he says. "It's older than me. Now, Boy," he says, "I need you to be a man and get me my revolver. It's on the shelf in my closet, just above my boots."

Henry's granddaddy was a Calvary Sergeant in the Confederacy. Picked up a Colt Army off a dead Union soldier at Stones River. When the war was over, he carried it everywhere he went. When Henry's daddy was born, Granddaddy Taylor went up to Chicago to work in the stockyards for a time, things being tough in Tennessee. Got into a bar fight with a couple of locals over a dollar in a game of Faro and one of the guys stabbed him in his right shoulder. Henry's granddad drew the pistol with his left hand and took down both of them before the other man could even draw his pistol. After that, he was on the run. He passed the revolver down to Henry's dad, Clay, and he passed it down to Henry. Henry gave me this pistol a while back to take care of for him, but he must've forgotten with all the medication. He does have another pistol, but it's not a revolver.

"Thought you said life was a poker game, not a crapshoot."

"Son, I'd rather play Roulette," he says.

"No, I can't do it."

"You can't or won't? If you ever loved me, you gotta do this. You pulled the trigger before, you can do it again, for me."

"No. Pistol's not here. Don't you remember?"

"Fucking pussy. Always thought you'd turn out a man but I see your panties showing. Makes me sick. Get your old man in here. He sure's shit better bring it to me."

A few months back, when I got into that big fight with mom, she told me it was her fault, the way I am. That she didn't have much time for me when I was a kid. I spent too much time around the wrong kind of people, men like Henry, who made me violent, angry, cynical, and cold-hearted. She's partly wrong. I'm not cold enough to pull the trigger on Henry, no matter what—or even to let him do it himself. Couldn't live with his blood on my hands. Even if I still had the pistol, I wouldn't bring it to Henry.

"What are you going to do, sit here and wait for me to die? Get the damn pistol or get to leaving. I've got to check out whether you help me or not, Son."

Dad and Grandma are talking to the nurse. Willa's her name—she's thin, has long, wavy blonde hair. She's about forty and really pretty, in a serious kind of way. Says she's going to quit cause Henry can't keep his hands off her. Grandma Clio says it's not true.

"He grabs my ass every time you leave the room. Even offered to marry me if he could get a piece of ass," the nurse says. She looks over at me and Tommy when she doesn't get sympathy from anyone else, then she looks away and shakes her head.

"Can't blame Henry. Way you're shaking your tail around here in that skirt, it's no wonder he's all wound up," Grandma says. "Henry's a handful, but he ain't that bad. You don't want to work here anymore, just say so."

"Dad, Henry wants you. He's asking for the revolver," I say.

"You got it, right?"

"Revolver's in a safe place. What about the .38?"

"Gave that to your Great Uncle Claude last year," Grandma says. "Found Henry passed out in his chair. Cigarette burning his finger in one hand, bottle of whiskey on the nightstand, and the .38 in his right hand, chamber open, box of shells spilled all over the floor and chair.

"Better hide all the pills around here," Willa says.

"No, if he does it, it won't be with pills. Gene, only gun we got left is the shotgun. Why don't you take that for now. I'll hide all the tow rope and clothesline, just in case."

"He won't do it himself," I say. "Wants me to do it."

"That old pervert grabs my crotch again, I'll finish him," Willa says. "Don't care how sick he is."

When I was sixteen, on my way to a school dance, Henry poured me a shot of Glenfiddich and told me, "There's three things you need to know in this life. Lose your temper, lose your edge. People are most often beat by themselves, by their own feelings and emotions. Best try not to feel." He poured us both another shot and slurred something about combing my hair. Then he said, "Dress tight. Good-looking gentlemen like you and me always get the girl if we look sharp and walk tall. Might not work at first, but eventually you win 'em over. Women judge everything on appearance."

He took another shot and sized me up. "Why you want to go to a dance dressed like a bum? Change into something respectable, Son. And one more thing, fail today, there's always tomorrow—till there's not."

I finished my shot and headed out the door without combing my hair or changing my clothes. All I said was, "Fail at what?" I didn't look back or wait for an answer. Grandma told me later on that Henry passed out in the recliner that night, waiting for me to get back. Charred his thumb and finger black cause somehow he held on to his cigarette passed-out and it burned down to the butt.

Me, Tommy and Dad take the long way home, the dirt roads around Raber and Stalwart. We drive past the fields and farms, around gravel road curves. The houses look abandoned, even though most aren't. Nobody says a word the whole time until we get to the main road.

"Let's not go home just yet," Dad says. He pulls into Ted's Country Store on the Meridian for a case of Busch.

"Do I get one?" Tommy asks him.

"No, you take the wheel. Billy and I are gonna get good and drunk." It's the first time Dad called me Billy since I was in the first grade.

"I was thinking, we should go out to the Carp tonight, or Nunns Creek. Dip some smelt," I say.

"Smelt aren't running good no more. Don't know if it's even worth it," Dad says. "Must've left the state with all the jobs a few years back." He laughs for a second, then his face gets real serious.

"We might do it, just for old times. Been a while," I say.

"Talked to your uncle Jack last night," he says.

"Still in Texas?"

"He's working the oil fields around McCook."

"I remember. It's not too far from McAllen," I say. "Stone throw from Mexico."

"You been there?" Tommy asks.

"Me, your brother and Jack made a trip down there when you were just a little shit."

"Don't remember much about Jack," Tommy says.

"Told him that they got DNA evidence on Cronin," Dad says. "Told me he wish he would've known that back then. Said he would've made the shot."

"What shot?" Tommy asks him.

Dad pulls off on a dirt road, one without a name, and tells us to get out. He grabs what's left of the case of beer and says, "Let's walk. This was your great grandparents' property. Ma just put it up for sale."

"I remember it," I say. "Used to be a barn over there."

"Shit—you do remember. Must've been about six, last time you were here."

The house is smaller than I remember and it's painted red. It used to be light green. Looks like the roof is in rough shape, all the old shingles hanging down from the front. Dad cracks a beer and hands one to me, then Tommy. We start off down a gravel road that curls around the clearing where the barn used to be. It turns into a grass path under the old, shady hardwoods.

"Lester Cronin has eighty acres of hunting property, looks a lot like this place, shares an access road with a big chunk of state land. The plan was, my buddy, Tony Vega, was gonna set up shop fifty yards from the road in a tree blind, right where Lester parked his truck and walked in to his blind. It would be the opening day of bow season, so we knew Lester Cronin would be out at his prime hunting property, in his lucky tree blind. We knew it was his favorite hunting spot cause he was such good friends with your grandpa Eddie and always talked about how many bucks he shot out there. Tony would wait there all day and split Lester's chest with an arrow when he came out of the woods. Tony was deadeye with any kind of weapon—hell, he probably could've taken Lester out at a hundred yards with a slingshot or a blowgun. Anyways, it would look like a hunting accident and there's no way anybody would suspect Tony. Nobody around town knew much about Tony except me, the rest of the family, and a few regulars from the Skunk House who'd never snitch on him. Besides, if things got hot, he was gonna run down to the Rio Grande Valley, maybe hop the border if he had to. We had it all planned out. Even bought arrows from Cronin's store. Thought it would make the revenge sweeter. Ironic, like the Colonel would say. Would've worked too, only problem, Tony started fucking that Canadian stripper again, Stacey."

"No, Lacey," I say.

"Then he blew his brains out and we had to go to plan B. Man I miss that fat son-of-a-bitch.

"Tony gone, somebody had to do something, so that's when Jack stepped up, said he could make the shot. Opening day, Jack waited all morning and no sign of Cronin. I dropped him off a half-mile from the road and he walked in through the woods so nobody who'd drive by know where he was going. All us Metzgers were the first suspects, anything happened to Lester, so we had to cover as many tracks as we could. Next day, same thing, Cronin's a no show. The pressure started getting to Jack—almost didn't go out after that, but we talked him into it. Then, on the third day, Cronin's old Chevy pick-up pulled in and Jack waited and watched. Almost fell asleep about the time Cronin came out the woods. Jack says he was listening to the classic rock station on his Walkman and that Zeppelin song, 'Ramble On,' came on right when he loosed the arrow from his quiver. He let fly and the arrow went about half a foot over Cronin's shoulder—real pisspoor shot. Not like Jack to miss, but he never shot at a person before. Got nervy.

"Just last year, Jack told me on the phone he was glad he missed Cronin. Nobody could say for sure he killed your Grandpa, so he would've felt guilty. He's thinking different now with that DNA evidence they got.

"Only took Cronin a couple seconds to unholster his .22 pistol and aim up the tree blind. Jack jumped down fifteen feet and run like hell. Didn't feel his sprained ankle till he got a good quarter mile from the blind. Cronin took off in his Chevy S-10. Looked to cut him off at the county road. Jack was smart. Stayed in the backwoods and headed north. Crossed the Meridian and came out by your Uncle Carl's place on Swede Road. Said he heard at least five .22 rounds ping by the trees around him when he was running.

"I saw Cronin drive by. I was cruising by every so often to pick up Jack. Figured the shit must've gone down bad when Cronin came out the road. That's when I knew we fucked up."

I remember when all this happened. Tommy was too young to remember much of it—showed on his face the whole time Dad was telling the story. Chad was out hunting with Lester that day and he told everybody at school about the stray arrow. He tested me, tried to get me to say something, but I kept quiet all day. Lester didn't know for sure who made the shot but he suspected it was either a Metzger or a LeVasseur. He just fired Jacques LeVasseur from the hardware store for being drunk a few days before Halloween. Jacques had nothing to lose so Lester figured he might come after him. Course, all us Metzgers had reason to go after him too. After Jack missed the shot, Chad Cronin ran his mouth more often, insulting Metzgers and LeVasseurs every chance he got. Nobody really liked Chad that much but he started having big parties at his place. The hardware store was making good money so he bought all kind of friends. Even though he was a weasel and a rat-faced momma's boy, he got popular in some circles, long as he was buying. Colonel Henry always says money is the great equalizer.

Dad cracks another Busch and tells Tommy to follow the path right on the fork in the grass road.

"Looks like nobody's been this way for a while," Tommy says.

Grass and weeds grow lawn tractor high down the middle and sides of the trail, but two lines of dirt mark years of tire wear.

"Good. Might find some morels down this way afore anybody else gets 'em," Dad says.

"Lucky I'm wearing my BDU pants," I say. "Cargo pockets should hold a few pounds of mushrooms."

Dad slaps me on the back and hands me the last beer from the case.

"Why don't I get that?" asks Tommy. "You guys been drinking all afternoon."

"This business with Cronin. It's over, Son," Dad tells me.

"Time to put all this shit behind us and get on to living. Couple years after the shot, I was at the Skunk House and Lester walked out back to take a piss in the woods. Thought about walking behind him and choking the life out the motherfucker. Maybe nobody would've ever known. In a way, I'm glad I didn't do it."

"Don't you hate him? You should've done it," I say.

"Some point, wasn't about Lester anymore. There's no bringing your grandpa Eddie back, so what's the point anyway."

"Goes deeper than that," I say. "Long as I live in this town I'll have to see Chad's face."

"Who's Chad? Cronin," Dad says. "Son, just cause he's Lester's grandson don't mean nothing. Shit, that boy ain't got nothing to do with it. You need to stop thinking crazy and get your act together."

"You're right," I tell him. "I'm done with the Cronins."

It's Saturday night. Johnny's home from Hillsdale for the semester so we hit the Channel Marker for a few drinks. Dad's already passed out or we would have drug him down there too. Haven't spent much time around town since I got back from the Army. Didn't really want to see people cause I just got back from Bosnia a few weeks before they sent me to Georgia to out-process. It's good to see some of the locals. Jay from my class and some of Johnny's school buddies had a few drinks with us so we got to tell Tommy some old sports stories and talk about the trouble we used to get in at school. Those guys have a softball tournament tomorrow so they didn't stay out too late. Invited me to join the team next year if I was still in town. Couple of Dad's work buddies bought me and Johnny a few rounds on their way out, left before we could repay the favor, so we're finishing up a couple mugs and a pitcher. Tommy's underage, so he gets to drive again. You'd think he'd be bored but he's getting a kick out of watching everybody get drunk, sipping a Coke. He's got a flask in the car though, so he's not sober, just less drunk than me and Johnny.

"Baseball coach down at Hillsdale asked about you again," Johnny says.

"He's getting too old for baseball," says Tommy.

"No, greatest shape of my life. Besides, not trying to go

pro—if I can get a scholarship at Hillsdale, I'd be set," I tell him. "Besides, might get my mind off everything, playing ball again."

"Shit, you ain't getting no baseball scholarship," Somebody says. We didn't even notice anybody was sitting by us. It's Chad Cronin. "Saw you play a couple games up at State. You couldn't hit for shit. How many fielding errors you make before they pulled you in that tournament up in Marquette?"

"Mind your fucking business, jackoff," I tell him. "We're not talking to you."

Then he makes that face he made when he'd see me in the halls at school. When he was telling everybody about how his grandpa Lester killed Grandpa Eddie.

"Let's finish these beers and get out of here," says Johnny. "Let's cruise out to Rockview so Tommy can have a few."

I clench my fists and stare down Chad. Johnny pats me on the back and rubs my shoulders when I slam my beer glass down on the oak bar.

"He's alright," Tommy tells Mike, the bartender, when he gives me that look like he's ready to call the cops faster than the town drunk can drop a pool chalk.

"Rockview? Going out to the cemetery to visit your gramps," Chad says when we're walking out the door. He laughs and gives us a look—like he still gets a sick thrill out of what Lester did. He looks half-retarded when he smiles and I want to knock his ass out but Johnny and Tommy push me through the door.

"No, we're gonna visit your gramps, douchebag. I hear he's up there now too," I tell him on my way out.

His face gets serious for a minute and then he shakes his head and goes back to his smirk and his Bacardi and Coke.

Johnny and Tommy walk me out toward the public dock. It's a clear night and the stars and three-quarter moon light up the bay. The southern wind chases away the chill for a few seconds and calms my throbbing temples. It's really good to be back home. The air is fresh and the tide from Lake Huron moves in smooth like dollar beer from the tap. The waves slap the dock and push back out toward the bay. I've been a lot of different places in the last few years and there's nothing compares to this—lakes like oceans where you can't see across to the other side, the evergreens, the birches, the cold, the comfort—I took it all for granted growing up here.

"Who the fuck was that guy?" Tommy asks.

"Chad Cronin," I say. "He used to brag around school that his grandpa killed Grandpa Eddie."

"Forget him," says Johnny. "Let's go drink some whiskey. This shit's over."

"Maybe not," I say. "Let's wait out here a while."

Johnny's always been the cool-headed one, the guy who cares about people, the brother who fixes the bad situations and tries to calm the rest of us down. But when it comes down to it, he's from the same mold as the rest of the family and he doesn't argue when I say we should stick around, even though the best thing for everybody would be to just go home and forget about Chad. Some shit is never over, though, and Tommy and Johnny know that, so they wait with me, let me make my play. We're all grown up but I'm still their big brother.

It's about 1:00 AM when Chad Cronin finally comes stumbling out the door. Didn't come with any friends and didn't leave with any, but he drunks struts out like he's leading the Fourth of July parade.

"Hey Chad," I say when he walks by on the sidewalk. "Saw your grandma Agnes the other day. She was giving head in the alley behind the feed store up in Pickford. Looked like she was sucking off a hog."

"What are you talking about you drunk fuck? Too much time in the Navy make you go crazy?"

"He was in the Army," Tommy tells him.

I grab Cronin's arm and start to pull. When he puts up a fight, I grab his throat and squeeze. Tommy grabs his back and looks around to make sure nobody's watching.

The waterfront's dead quiet. All the lights are out and we're in the shadowy area of the parking lot.

"What the fuck are you guys doing?" Johnny says. He half looks worried and half-laughs.

"I was just messing around. It's all in good fun," I say. "Right Chad? Let's give Chad a shot." I let go of Chad's throat and grab the hood of his sweatshirt, pull it down to the small of his back, then use it to control him like a leash on a dog.

We walk past the barber shop, the barber pole turning in circles, the only light on the lakeshore side of the street past the bar. Half the buildings and houses that've been on this street for a century are run-down now. Some look empty. When we were kids, there were more people around. Now everything is closed down. The Bon Air is part-covered in tar paper. They only open for ice cream in the summer now, Mom told me.

When we get to the car, in the dark street shadows, I tell Tommy to get the bottle of Kessler's.

"Take a shot," I tell Tommy. "And how 'bout you Cronin. Want a drink?"

"I don't drink that cheap shit," he says. "What the fuck you want? You guys done? Had about enough of this bullshit. Lucky if I don't call my lawyer."

"We all know your grandpa Lester killed our grandpa Eddie. That funny to you?"

He shakes his head no but he's got that same look, like he's trying not to laugh. I slap his face the way you tap a dog's nose when he shits on the floor. Then I slap him again, hit him harder, and I can't tell if he's smiling or trying not to cry.

"I'm glad Grandpa Lester killed your faggot grandpa. What you going to do about it?"

He starts to kick at Tommy and me when we grab his arms. Johnny has some trouble with the trunk key but he finally wiggles it open. Cronin hears the trunk pop and he really starts to panic and scream. I bitchslap him across the face and he screams louder. I ask Johnny and Tommy if they can get his legs and they nod. I grab him by the hood of his sweatshirt and twist with my right hand until it starts to choke him. His face turns pale-red and he tries to kick harder but Tommy and Johnny each got a leg. Johnny punches behind Cronin's knee with his left hand. I cover his mouth and he tries to bite my hand. I ram his head into the open trunk lid and tell Tommy to take out the tire iron. When Cronin sees Johnny with the iron he drops and cowers into a back corner of the trunk. When we close the trunk, he bangs and screams for a while and then he starts to cry, begging for help. Johnny turns up the radio. He's got

Hank Williams in the tape deck and the deep vocal tracks cover Chad's screaming from the trunk. We drive around the block, past the school, past the community center and the grocery store and turn north on the Meridian, out toward Rockview Hill.

When we were younger, Dad always protected Johnny and Tommy from trouble. I got involved in a lot more since I was the oldest. One time, day before Christmas Eve, Tony came back all bloody and drunk and Dad was so drunk he couldn't walk. They didn't want Mom to know so they woke me up to help. Had to grab towels and peroxide. Dad made me drive from our house to Tony's apartment. I was only thirteen. By the time we got home, only had three hours to sleep, but I kept rolling around in bed and then Mom told us to get up and shovel out the driveway. I asked for help and they were going to send out Johnny until he started faking sick, coughing and sniffling, so Mom kept him in. On my way back outside, he stuck his tongue out at me while he sat there with Tommy, watching cartoons and sipping cocoa. I told Dad I was going to snitch on him if he didn't pay up. He gave me five bucks that I used to buy .410 shells, but I would have traded ten to shower Tony's blood off my arms and crawl back into bed. That kind of thing happened all the time back then but Johnny and Tommy didn't see it, not like I did.

We stopped at the gas station on the way out of town, paid double the cost for duct tape and a two-hundred-foot bundle of clothesline rope. I parked away from the store and we turned up the radio so nobody could hear Cronin if he started to scream again. Ran into Blake Braune at the gas station. He was on duty so I was kind of paranoid talking to him. All he said was I looked drunk and he hoped I wasn't driving. I told him Tommy was and he laughed and got back into his county patrol car. By the time we got to the graveyard, Chad already kicked a couple dents in the top of the trunk. Glad the only cop we saw was Blake.

Chad's tied to an oak tree next to Lester Cronin's grave, a tree that's been there for at least a hundred years before the cemetery. We didn't tie Chad up right away—had to beat him down a while before we could get the rope on him. He tried to run away but Johnny ran up behind him and tackled him, knocked him into the top bar of the steel fence that corrals the graves, so Chad's face is bloody and his eye sockets are dark blue in the lantern light. His arms are stretched out behind his back, bound by cord and duct tape. We used all the tape, all the rope and our best Boy Scout knots. From his neck to his nose, Cronin looks like a duct-taped Egyptian mummy. Even his ankles are taped together.

I position the lantern so Cronin can see the show. When Johnny and Tommy start to piss, the water shines bright golden yellow in the fluorescent light. It settles and foams over Lester's name and date of birth.

"Hurry, you're going to miss it," Tommy tells me.

"Thought the three of us gonna do this together," Johnny says.

I unzip and Cronin squirms as much as he can tied down. Mostly just his face twists and stretches, wrinkling the duct tape. It's dark but I can see my urine glow in the shadows, dark yellow, almost brown, from all the beer and vodka shots and whiskey. Been drinking since the dawn cracked. Letting loose is the most beautiful relief. The waiting, the build-up, was almost painful and it stings as much as it soothes, the longer I go but I can't stop—I feel Cronin's pain with every second the golden water douses his clothes. I aim up toward his neck, and hair, and cover as much of his body as I can.

"You're born again," I tell him. "Into a world of piss."

He squirms and wriggles when the moisture rolls through the tape around his mouth. When the pressure lessens I wet his jeans and shoes, his feet in an acid puddle at the base of the oak. When this is over, he might try to get revenge but he'll have to go it alone. No way he'll admit to anybody what happened here.

My brothers' faces sober watching me, seeing Chad's face. I was only supposed to piss on the grave like Johnny and Tommy but I changed the plan without telling myself. In a way, I'm sorry for Chad—Lester brought him into this just like he brought in the rest of us.

Chad drips and shivers and stinks in the glow of lantern light. The white of his shirt is stained the color of rotgut.

"You and me, we're all even now, far as I'm concerned. All these years, running your mouth, bragging about your grandpa Lester. It's done. Think hard about your next step, Chad. You're the last of the line when it comes to Cronins. I'll let you go about your business, long as you never pull the kind of shit old Lester did.

Just remember something—there's plenty of Metzgers around these parts. Anything you start, we can end it. I'll end it."

I cut the duct tape that covers his mouth with a jackknife Grandpa Eddie gave me. It's a four-inch blade with an ivory-colored handle and black etchings of trophy bucks. Justice would have been to stick it in Lester Cronin's chest and watch him bleed out.

"Tell me, Cronin, give me a reason to cut these ropes."

I rip the wet tape from his mouth.

"Fuck you."

"That's not the answer we're looking for. A guy like me, Chad—I'll never sleep sound again. Doesn't matter to me one way or another if you're around or not."

Breakfast in Tennessee smells like home, like the old-time breakfasts at Grandpa Eddie and Grandma Gloria's house, except they serve links here instead of kielbasa and there's grits instead of potatoes, just like when I was stationed in Georgia. First time I ate grits, back in basic training, I sprinkled sugar on them. You would've thought I killed somebody. The boys from Georgia, Alabama and Mississippi said it was just wrong in all kind of ways, that they had a lot to teach me about southern living. I know better now. If I look out of place in this roadside diner, it's because of the book in front of me, not the way I eat. Started reading the Nietzsche Colonel Henry gave me a couple days ago. Soon as I opened it, I found the letter to me in the back. I left right away to take care of his business in Tennessee. Didn't even wait for the funeral. Funny thing, the Colonel marked some of his favorite parts of the book with pages from the Bible—underlined some of his favorite quotes in the book and on the Bible pages in pencil and black pen. On the page where he left the letter, he underlined a part that talks about joy wants deep eternity. Didn't make much sense to me—figured it might be a bad translation—but Henry thought it was important, so I'll give it a better look when I get a chance.

In the back of the book there was a folded map of the old Dixie Highway route. I've been following some of those roads on the way down.

Snow fell when I crossed the Mackinac Bridge. I drove two hours with the window down so the cold air would keep me awake.

There wasn't any snow past Flint. Hard to believe how much warmer it is in Tennessee—must be 60 degrees. The hills and flatlands are a dull green and flowers bloom all along the highway. There's mist over the canyons and white bright clouds in the baby blue sky, just the way I remember it from that trip I made down to Texas with Uncle Jack and Dad.

Maybe I'll track down Jack in the Rio Grande Valley when I'm done in Tennessee. Grandpa Mike is in Florida, somewhere by Miami, on the other end of Henry's Dixie Highway map. I could try to find him too. Got Army buddies all over the country. Might head down to Mississippi and work with Hal Killegrew laying brick. He always said there was a job waiting for me down in Stone County if I didn't mind breaking my back.

I left Michigan early yesterday morning. Didn't tell my parents or Tommy. Johnny went back to Hillsdale for a couple days to see his basketball coach. He's starting point guard next season so he says he needs more time with the playbook. Maybe he just needed to get away from home for a while. Before I left, I drove by Grandma Gloria's place and a light was on in the kitchen so I pulled in. Uncle Ray had a wheelbarrow full of gravel and was filling in driveway mud ruts. He didn't stop shoveling the whole time he told me about the firewood business he started up. He said I could work with him, save up money for school whenever I wanted.

Thought about going into the house, saying goodbye to Grandma Gloria, but Ray and I both thought she'd be asleep. When I left, I saw her standing by the window, cup of coffee in one hand and a brown cigarette in the other. I pretended not to see her, but we made eye contact for a few seconds before I turned away and opened the car door. I think she saw my face long enough for her to read the truth about me, see my shame, so I turned to the Buick and drove out her gravel driveway without looking back. A light snow started up when I drove past Hessel, but the sun still tried to peek through the mix of puffed gray and white clouds. I kept the window down all the way to the Mackinac Bridge to stay awake. My breath fogged the air over the dashboard. The wind would blow in and whistle in my left ear until that side of my face and neck got numb—my legs and right side burned from the heat blasting through the floor and dash. My driving foot tired and tingled asleep, my sock sweaty on the gas pedal. The cruise control broke like they always do in older cars on long trips, when you need it most. I tried to click it on a few times but it wouldn't catch, so I punched the windshield and cranked up the classic rock station for a while until every song started to sound the same and I switched to the station from Interlochen and heard Mozart's Piano Concerto No 21, music we used to listen to while we painted in Mrs. Gurov's Art class. The melody and the memory put me in a trance so I cracked the window again and shocked myself awake to drums and rock guitars, shouting out songs that have no real meaning to me, till my voice tired and I banged the steering wheel like a drum to feel like I wasn't alone, like I wasn't traveling down a highway to the what was not known and maybe into a whole hell of a lot of trouble. Didn't stop until just past Bay City, on the way into Saginaw. There was a bottleneck right up to the Zilwaukee Bridge and I saw the overpasses and green highway markers up close, the Chevys, the Fords, the Dodges and GMs, all starting to peel, Michigan rusting all around me and I don't think I noticed it before, when I was young, before I left for the Army but it all started happening a while back, I think—I'm sure.

By Saginaw, all the snow was gone. I trashed my empty half-gallon bottle of Kessler's at a Marathon station, traded down for sixteen ounces of black coffee and a half-dozen box of stale cake donuts, and stashed a twelve-pack of Busch in the trunk for later. By then the bright cold sun poked through the clouds and stung my tired eyes but I kept on, weaving and dodging through angry morning traffic in Detroit and the lunch-time rush over the Maumee River in Toledo. I stopped off for a burger in Bowling Green and saw a girl who looked like Katherine Beckett, but wasn't. I kept on south until I fell asleep at the wheel at dusk but the shoulder gravel spooked me and I yanked the wheel straight before I might've rammed a rural overpass between cities on I-75. That got me to thinking that maybe Ronnie LeVasseur didn't do himself in—maybe he was just in a bad way—or maybe just driving tired. Three hours after dark, somewhere south of Ohio's Kentucky border, I pulled into a rest area, took my dinner from a vending machine, washed it down with a few beers from the twelve-pack in my trunk and slept bent-kneed in my car.

JOSEPH DANIEL HASKE

Photo by Richard Coronado

Joseph D. Haske chairs the English Department at South Texas College, where he has taught for the past ten years. He was awarded the 2011 *Boulevard* Emerging Writers prize for short fiction and his work is featured in various anthologies and in journals such as *Boulevard*, *Pleiades*, the *Texas Review*, *AleCart*, *Romania Literara*, *Rampike*, the *Four-Way Review*, *Boema*, *Convorbiri Literare*, *Paradigma* and *Fiction International*. He lives in Mission, Texas with his wife, Bertha, and their children, Ferny and Joey.